Bird

of

Dereliction

By

Charlie

Selkirk

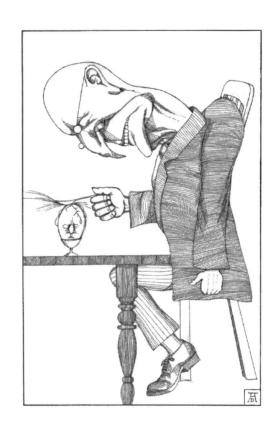

CONTENTS

Published in the UK by Dr Aquaspine Publishing

draquaspinepublishing@aol.com

draquaspinepublishing.co.uk

First Printing December 2022

ISBN: 978-1-7398014-0-3

Illustrations by The Author

Acknowledgements and Thanks to

Laura Howell for Cover & Book Design

Cathy Howell and Andy Sykes for Invaluable Support

Dr Aquaspine Publishing

To the memory of Timmy the Crab.
Whose brief but courageous life ended on
Bridlington Beach in the summer of 1963.
May his tiny exoskeleton rest in peace.

The Vendor

I approached the house on a starlit night, clutching the brochure.

Three up, two down, modern semi.

As I opened the front gate a savage-looking dog appeared in an upstairs window. A reflection of the moon in the glass shone just above the dog creating the illusion that the house contained nothing but a bleak, endless prairie.

I walked up the path and the dog began a frenzied barking.

Before I reached the door it was already opening and the vendor was benevolently waving me in rather like a lifeboatman saving a stricken sailor.

'When you have a dog like mine you don't really need a doorbell.'

Apprehensively I stepped into the hall.

'Please don't mind Fletcher, all the usual stuff applies. You know, his bark is worse than his bite; he's only saying hello; he's more scared of you than you are of him, etcetera, etcetera. He's one of those dogs that if you're downstairs he's upstairs, if you're in one room then he's in another, if you're inside then he's outside. Let's say, he makes his presence felt without actually being there.'

I certainly had the feeling that Fletcher was watching me although I couldn't actually locate him.

'I have been informed that the house is completely empty and that there is no chain.'

'You have been informed correctly. My wife left me after the premature demise of our son. She always blamed me for the death but nothing is ever as black and white as that. She's now living with a commercial traveller called Bunt. Obviously with the break-up of the marriage I've had to sell the house. I also have found new love. I'm living with the rather comely lady in her flat above the butcher's shop. I'm certain the location guarantees a varied and full diet. It will be good for Fletcher too, if I can manage to prise him away from this place. I suppose I got Fletcher, in a manner of speaking, to replace my son. He has been a handful, but I suppose that has helped to distract me from my grief. So yes, the house is empty as far as possible. Yet, who can make such a claim with absolute certainty? There may be the odd fingernail clipping trapped in the gap between the floorboards. There may be one or two oddments we've missed, but apart from that, as far as is humanly possible, the house is definitely empty.'

It was as if, in the vendor's state of grief, an invisible elastic had snapped, leaving the flesh over the abdomen hanging like an empty pouch.

'Well. Shall we begin at the outside, meander inside and then steadily work our way upward. Or, on the other hand, shall we make a sharp, preliminary ascension, work our way gradually downward and then move to the outside. It's completely up to you. The latter would give more opportunity for a quick getaway at the end of the course.'

He smacked his hands together and started to rub them vigorously.

'We'll start with the upstairs.'

'Ah, you're going for the quick getaway.'

'Well, no, not really it's …'

We started to climb the stairs. The vendor began his interrogation.

'So you're moving then. Alone? Married? Children? Ageing parents? Nephews? Nieces? Or are you building a secret love nest? Or maybe a hideaway for a drugs racket? Or a terrorist bomb factory?'

'No, just the wife and two kids. Our present house is too small. We're looking for something bigger.'

'What is it? Boy, boy? Girl, girl? Girl, boy? Boy, girl?'

'Girl, boy.'

'You specifically want to move into this area?'

'Well I do, but my wife would rather move into the country.'

'Is that a sign of conflict in the marriage? A little fissure? The fissures have a habit of accumulating until you have a major continental drift. The children are swallowed in the stormy waters that intervene. Maybe you're already starting to compensate by having affairs on the side. Got your eye on the rather attractive girl that works in the accounts department?'

'No, it's nothing like that. It's just a very minor difference of opinion.'

The vendor snorted.

I hoped by now that we were nearly at the top of the stairs. My view ahead was limited by the steady swaying of the vendor's enormous arse. I looked backwards down the stairs and discovered that we had gone less than a third of the way. I tried to change the subject but I couldn't manage to project a different perspective beyond the object that heaved before me.

'Do you ever wonder what your wife saw in you? I suppose you were a younger man. Thinner. No sagging. White teeth. Clean underpants. God, look at us now. No wonder they're dissatisfied.'

We continued to rise. The echo of the heavy footsteps of the vendor in the empty house sounded like a pile driver pulsing in the distance.

'Mind you, the ladies fare no better. Don't you find that vivacious freshness they have in their late teens and early twenties fades rapidly. The first sign of the gradual landslide towards the menopause. It's a tragedy. I find as I grow older I can see into the future. Quite often I can look at teenage girls and visualise the old hags they will eventually become. At first I perceive what may be a pretty face that looks as if it will last forever. Then I notice a slight beakiness of the nose, or a slight heaviness of the skin below the chin, or a hint of the flesh above the eye sagging. Then I think ahhhh.'

At last we reached half-way.

'So, were you a virgin when you married? No, of course not. How many girls did you have? One? Two? Three? Ten? Twenty? Thirty?'

'I really can't remember.'

'Ha. I thought you'd say something like that. 'I can't remember,' or, 'A few but I can't recall exactly how many'. Of course you can remember. You can recount, in vivid detail, each one. Go on, how many? I'm not asking you to name them. You can make the number up if you really want.'

'No, I really can't remember.'

'The problem is that you are uncertain as to what the correct protocol is. Does the stigma lie with the Don Juan or the perennial non-starter? I suppose in the circumstances it might be best to claim, not too many, not too few. Mind you, today kids have more sex before the legal age than I ever had after it. Find they've got an erection, ram it home and then they think they're in love. Still, in the main, it's all over for us. You've had your family, why should nature continue to provide you with a sex life? I'll wager you're having difficulty getting a decent stiffy nowadays. When was the last time you had satisfactory rumpypumpy?

The vendor's line of conversation had just about exhausted my patience.

"I mean, are you a ten time a night man? A once a weeker? A twice a yearer? A decader? Or has it all just petered out altogether?"

Fortunately we reached the top of the stairs.

"Ah, here we are."

We stood in darkness on the landing as the vendor fumbled for the light switch.

"Funny really, however long you've lived in a place it doesn't guarantee you actually know it that well."

The light came on.

"Well, as you can see, it's all very compact. Two decent size bedrooms, a box room and a combined bathroom and toilet. Shall we start with the box room?"

We shuffled into the box room, the vendor looked a little surprised.

"There you are, certainly box-like, but it's not as small as you might have imagined. Oh dear, we seem to have left what looks like a toy cupboard with all its contents. I assure you that before the exchange of contracts it will have been removed."

I felt something more needed saying.

"It's not so much the toy cupboard, but the small boy playing with the toys."

"Yes, of course, you're right. I'm not sure what he's doing here actually. This small oversight will be put right. He seems rather isolated and lonely. A little like myself as a child perhaps. Oh what toss. We always do that don't we. We like to pretend that we're formed from all the hardships of life, don't we. 'Nobody really knows me'. 'It was a long, heroic struggle to become the person I am.' 'I'm a tortured, misunderstood soul.' 'I've always been an outsider.'"

We stepped over the toys scattered across the floor.

"You'll find it hard to believe, but I was a bullying little shit when I was young. In a sense I probably was isolated, but with good reason. Nobody liked me. I'm not sure who this boy is though. Just for a second, I thought he was my son."

The vendor walked to the window and pointed to the array of bright points of light as if it was a pre-arranged diversion.

"Anyway, you get a good view from here. In daylight you can see the abattoir, the tannery, the dog food factory, the cat food factory, the fertiliser factory, and the glue factory where all the left-over bits of animal are boiled down to make a particularly excellent adhesive. It's reassuring to know it's all out there, functioning busily, wheels within wheels, safe as houses. I must admit you do get a bit of a whiff if the wind's in the wrong direction."

We turned round to leave. I saw squarely into the toy cupboard, giving a glimpse of the child's world.

The ascent of the shelves formed a facsimile of the stages of prehistory. Models of reptiles wandered through the Triassic and Jurassic eras, perished in the Cretaceous and were replaced by mammals in the Cenozoic. The top of the cupboard was filled with the black of the cosmos to be penetrated by an impressive collection of plastic rockets.

The vendor returned from the window. As he passed the boy he absent-mindedly patted him on the head.

"Never mind. Egg on chin. Egg on chin. We'll sort it all out."

Back on the landing, the vendor stood before the closed door of one of the other bedrooms.

"This is a good-size room that looks out onto the street."

Tentatively he opened the door as if he feared that this may also contain something that should have already been removed.

To his obvious relief the room was completely empty. We walked across the bare floorboards.

"This room is easily big enough to have …"

A siren sounded in the street and an urgent blue light flickered on the walls. The vendor groaned.

"That this should have happened while you were here. If it only could have waited until the contract had been signed."

We looked out of the window. A fire engine had drawn up to the next door neighbour's house on the side of the adjoining wall. As flames burst through the doors and windows I could see people climbing down the walls on knotted sheets. As they accumulated in the front garden they began a noisy disputation, I presumed they had already begun the task of dispensing the blame.

"They're always having fires. Sometimes a period of a month or two passes without, but then sometimes it happens two or three times in a week. I'm afraid this probably detracts slightly from the selling points of the house."

"Shouldn't we be getting out? Aren't we in some danger if we stay here?"

The vendor seemed fairly cool about the matter.

"No, no. The fire never gets through. The brave boys in uniform so far have always managed to put it out in good time. Thus I have no doubt that they will always continue to do so, ad infinitum."

The vendor pointed to the bedroom wall.

"Sometimes you can feel hotspots but the fire never spreads. Please don't let this minor occurrence affect your decision to move here."

I touched the wall, in some parts the wall was hotter than my hand could bear.

Outside, the group of victims had been joined by various officials. I could see fire-brigade chiefs and police sergeants adding their voices to arguments.

"They always blame each other. They're always changing the fire regulations but it never improves things. The amended rules always contain some loop-holes, or subtle contradictions."

"But they always manage to get them out, before it's too late."

"Oh, no, no. It's all too often the fate of whole families to be torched to death. Most of the time it ends in tragedy. But as I say, don't let this worry you too much. It's the neighbour's concern, not ours. Let them get on with it. It's absolutely nothing whatsoever to do with this house. We've never been so careless as to let a fire start here, I trust future occupiers will do all in their power to do likewise.

We started to withdraw from the room. The vendor continued his reassuring conversation.

"Anyway, nowadays we usually have to put up with problem neighbours. We must learn to become stoics. Not let ourselves be put off too much when we consider the purchase of new properties."

We stood outside the third bedroom.

The vendor seemed much more confident, as if he felt the main problem areas had been covered and from now on it was plain sailing.

With a grand sweep of his arm he opened the door.

"This bedroom is slightly bigger than the other one. It looks out onto the back garden. Since it's away from the street it's the quietest room. If I was you I'd bag this room. It's also got an airing cupboard. So if you have a heavy night on the beer you can dry your pants off here."

As he continued his banter he stood in the doorway with his back to the room. Behind him I could see a large bed with a man and a woman sleeping on it.

The vendor turned round. He partially hid his grimace behind his hand.

It seemed relevant to inquire who the people were.

"I must admit I'm not altogether sure."

The vendor cautiously peeled back the bedclothes. The man remained in his deep slumber, I noticed his body was covered in silver streaks. I could have imagined these were the trails of slugs that had traversed his torso with the velocity of race horses compared with the man's impressive state of inertia.

"I think they are friends of my wife. They may have been called the Hicks or the Higgs, or possibly something completely different. It was years ago that they visited. I must admit that for quite a long time I have been preoccupied with various problems, particularly my son's death, but you think I would have noticed that they never left. If I remember correctly they were rather a vile, indolent pair, maybe it's not all that surprising that they are still here."

Mr Higgs started to snore loudly which woke Mrs Higgs up.

She failed to notice that two men were standing beside the bed, but instead spied the slime covering the man.

"You've been masturbating. You've been masturbating, in secret while I've been asleep."

Mr Higgs stirred.

"What?"

"You've wanked surreptitiously."

"I've been asleep all the time."

Mrs Higgs screamed.

"How could you do this? You've been unfaithful to me in your dreams. Who is she? How often has this been happening? Why? Why? Why?"

She jumped out of bed and started to throw her shoes at Mr Higgs.

Mr Higgs defended himself with his crooked arm. He sat upright, suddenly lurched forward and caught his wife by the elbows in mid-throw. He managed to pull her towards himself as his head was subjected to a cascade of blows from Mrs Higgs clenched fists. His right hand came up sharply and struck her on the side of her face with a loud slap.

Mrs Higgs stopped. For several seconds, barely moving, she stared at him. Then their mouths clamped hard together like two over-powered vacuum pumps and Mr Higgs penis started to slide like a worm across the sheets towards Mrs Higgs.

I felt the vendor's hand on my shoulder propelling me back towards the door.

"I think matters are getting out of hand here. Maybe we'll pop back later and have a proper look at the room. That is, if you're still interested. I must admit it all seems a little animalistic. Still, if the walls of people's houses were suddenly removed we'd all be caught fornicating and shitting like the beasts in the fields."

We came to the bathroom. This was located at the top of the stairs.

"I'm afraid there's nothing exotic here. No sunken bath or even a bidet."

He pushed on the door but it appeared to have jammed.

"The only drawback is the ventilation brick above the lavatory. In the winter the wind whistles through, making a rather morbid, wailing sound."

He pushed harder on the door but it still failed to open.

"I always think it sounds like the souls of Fletcher's ancestors crying to be let in. If it bothered you too much you could always Sellotape it over. You know the door seems to have stuck a bit. I'm going to have to put my shoulder to it."

I felt I had to offer what was becoming a rather increasingly obvious explanation.

"Maybe there's somebody inside."

The vendor frowned.

"Really? Does that seem likely?"

I declined to respond.

"I know, I'll try the old trick of peeking under the door."

He went a short distance down the stairs as if he was going down a ladder. When his eyes were on a level with the bottom of the door, he stopped.

"Well certainly either side of the bit of the lavatory that screws to the floor, I can see what appears to be a pair of slippers. In fact they seem to be those awful tartan slippers with fluffy bits near the top. In fact they seem to be the same kind of slippers that my father used to …'

Troubled, the vendor came back up the stairs. Reverently he tapped on the door.

"Dad? Dad are you still in there?"

There was no response.

The vendor pressed his ear to the door.

"Is that you in there Dad?"

The vendor indicated for me to listen.

"There's a sound, only just audible, coming from within. What do you make of it?"

I could hear faint music. It sounded as if an orchestra had been trapped in an airtight container.

"I think it might be light opera."

"Of course. It'll be Gilbert and Sullivan. He must have head-phones on. In that case we'll never get through. I think we're going to have to give the bathroom a miss as well I'm afraid. In a sense you might say he's trapped in there by his music. Oh yes, and his ongoing problem with constipation. Given his unexpected presence here, it's probably the best place for him. If it's alright with you I'd rather leave him in there. The thought of him roaming free is infinitely undesirable. I'm terribly sorry, but it seems you've chosen a rather unfortunate time to see the house."

We tackled the descent of the stairs. On the ascent my world-view had been limited to the vendor's posterior, now it was open to the top of his head. As the vendor resumed his interrogative conversation, at least my location was less claustrophobic.

"So your wife wants to live in the country but you, I gather, do not?"

"It would be further to travel to work."

"I see. Is your wife one of those people who envisage a return to nature? Start it all again from the beginning and all that? The urge to find Utopia?"

"Well not really. She thinks it would be a cleaner, safer environment. Better for the kids I suppose."

"Ah yes. It would probably have been better for my son. He would have liked it as well. He was a plucky little chap. Wasn't scared of anything. Well, almost nothing. I believe at the most there was one thing that he was scared of. It would be better for Fletcher as well. As we go for walks along the streets, the turds he deposits on the pavement look so out of place. If he was out in the countryside it would be a different matter. He could partake in the cycles of nature. Fletcher would become a valid source of fertility. You haven't seen Fletcher by any chance have you? I wonder where he has got to? Fletcher? Fletcher?"

As the vendor rambled on, I began to wonder whether to abandon this viewing. When we reached the bottom of the stairs, it might have seemed more honest to give my apologies and simply leave by the front door without seeing the rest of the house. The vendor may have guessed my intention by the rather brief, uninterested answers I was giving to his endless questions.

"I implore you not to judge the quality of the house by these faux pas. I do understand. I'm totally on your side. When anybody wants to move house they expect to start again from scratch. They want to put in their own furniture, choose their own wallpaper and not have the previous occupier's personal belongings, curtains, kitchen sinks, parents, friends, unidentified children blocking the place up."

On the way up the stairs the journey had been interminable. I noticed on the way down we were beginning to accelerate.

"I guarantee that everything will be sorted out. I assure you that there is no problem here. Besides there is still a lot more to see. In the back garden there is a particularly interesting feature that you definitely must not miss."

We were going faster and faster. When we reached the bottom of the stairs I tried to continue in a straight line towards the front door. The vendor had anticipated my manoeuvre. He linked arms and, utilising my increased momentum, swung me almost in a complete circle so that I was now moving up the hall but in the opposite direction from the front door.

"I always try to convince myself that however bad something has turned out, something much worse could have happened."

We came to a sudden stop outside the door of the front room.

"For instance we could have bumped into my paternal and maternal grandparents."

He opened the door. The room was completely filled with old people. From the vendor's face I could see that they were familiar to him.

They appeared to be watching a war film on the biggest television set I'd ever seen. As soon as the vendor opened the door they started to make demands on him.

"Switch up the sound, I can't hear."

The vendor obediently crossed the room to the television set.

"Have you switched up the sound yet, I'm a little deaf."

The vendor switched the sound up further.

"It's really not loud enough, switch it up higher."

The vendor switched the sound up even further.

"I can still hardly hear it."

The vendor continued to turn the volume control. By now it sounded as if the war was actually being conducted in the room.

"Higher."

"Higher."

"Higher."

"Higher."

The knob reached its natural limit.

"Higher."

"Higher."

"Higher."

"Higher."

I could see the vendor frantically twisting the knob.

"Higher."

"Higher."

"Higher."

"Higher."

"It won't go any bloody higher you old ratbags."

The vendor was yelling as loud as he could. The ensuing wave of discontent was absorbed in a startling round of machine gun fire.

To my surprise I looked at the screen and realised that it showed an image of the vendor himself clutching his abdomen as the entirety of his intestinal tract slithered from a gaping wound between the top of his trousers and his shirt. The gunfire stopped and the vendor collapsed forward into the heap of bloody entrails before him. For a second everything went quiet then a load unanimous cheer went up from the old people.

The vendor pushed his way back across the room as the picture on the screen switched to new battlefields. The gunfire resumed.

I noticed the old people were frantically dabbing their fore-fingers on the buttons of devices clutched in their shaking hands.

When the vendor reached me he seemed quite angry.

"They think they are making factual reconstructions of their lives, loves, wars, victories and God knows what. What the stupid twats forgot is that they are just manipulating everything with their remote controls."

He slammed the door shut behind him.

"Look, I'm sorry that was just appalling. How can I apologise? I think it might be a good time to simply terminate this appointment now and forget all about it."

I felt a little sorry for the vendor.

"Look, I do understand. You've just gone through a difficult time, what with the death of your son and the divorce. I can see you've been under pressure and things have gone a bit astray. I would like to look at the rest of the house. I am very much looking forward to seeing the unusual feature in the back garden."

The vendor looked a little less agitated.

"Thank you for being so understanding, that makes things a lot easier. Of course, I was just being silly. You're right, things have been difficult."

He blew his nose into a large handkerchief and apart from his eyes looking a little watery and red, he had regained his composure.

"For a second there I lost my perspective. There is nothing for me to worry about. All the problems here are remnants from the past. My father, the seemingly endless quantity of grandparents, the Higgs ..."

Just as the vendor mentioned the Higgs, they emphasised their presence with a spectacular mutual orgasm.

"... the Higgs. They are all from the past. They will all quickly fade away in time. That is apart from the lonely, young boy in the box room. But I think I remember who he is. I believe he is the Higg's son. But I certainly don't think they've had any more children, they've been indulging in too much sex to have children. So apart from the solitary presence of the young boy which might be a bit problematical ..."

The vendor opened the door to the kitchen.

The kitchen was jammed full with children. They appeared to be having a party. We squeezed through at the back just as 'Uncle Horace's Magic Show' was getting into full swing.

Uncle Horace ejected fire from his mouth, but the inflammable liquid scorched his lips so the show had to be interrupted as he applied Vaseline to the burnt areas. Uncle

Horace produced a white dove from his sleeve, but something snapped as he was pulling it out. He threw the bird into the air, but instead of achieving flight it fluttered miserably to the floor, its wing hanging pitifully down, obviously broken. Uncle Horace conjured a rabbit from his top hat, but sadly it had asphyxiated.

The magic show over, the cake was brought in. It was divided with time-honoured fairness. The attractive children and ebullient children received the largest portions. The nonentitous little urchins near the back received the smaller portions cut from the hard periphery of the cake.

Finally it was time for Uncle Horace to ignite the sparklers.

Uncle Horace stepped forward drunkenly with his cigarette lighter.

The children queued with their unlit sparklers. One little girl proudly wearing her best party frock stepped forward. As the little girl held her sparkler in the flame, Uncle Horace hiccoughed causing the lighter to jerk.

The front of the little girl's dress caught alight, a circle of flames rapidly spread out. Whimpering, she tried to flap out the flames with her hand, but the sleeve caught fire. She held up the arm as if she was appealing for someone to take away the fire. The children around her quickly scattered. With horrific speed she became a hopeless inferno.

There was no time to act before the flames and the child disappeared into a few puffs of pure, white vapour. The rest of the children began to howl and Uncle Horace fainted. Only the vendor remained enthusiastic.

"Well. What a remarkable trick. I thought this was the typical, drab children's party as I always remembered them, in fact as recorded in history from the beginning of time. How wrong I was. The kiddies won't forget that one in a hurry. And I'd always thought of Uncle Horace as a mediocre magician. Now I realise he should be up there with the all-time greats."

As we stepped out of the kitchen I was personally in a state of shock.

"Are you sure that wasn't for real and, despite your claims earlier, that you never had fires, you've just had one and apparently didn't notice.'

"Oh, no, no. It was a clever illusion, a sleight-of-hand. What are you trying to do? Resurrect my memories of my dead son? Torture me with my feelings of guilt and regret? It was a sleight-of-hand that's all. There is nothing more to the matter."

I turned back to the kitchen one more time and saw the mayhem of crying children. Uncle Horace was back on his feet but reeling like a detached rotor.

We passed from the kitchen into an annexe that had been converted for use as a wash-room. The vendor waved his hand towards the comprehensive range of washing machines, spin driers and tumble driers.

"It is of course extremely convenient to have an area designed solely for washing clothes."

"But the machines appear to be in operation."

The vendor bent over the nearest machine. Garments rotated within the circular window.

"Oh yes. Now you mention it, I can't remember a time when they haven't been in operation. Pumping away endlessly. They must have shifted tons of dirty clothes. After a time I suppose you cease to hear the constant clanking and whirring. I'm terrible with this sort of thing. I haven't the faintest how to switch them on and have only the vaguest idea what each machine actually does."

As we walked past the machines to the back door, a flux of people were either pushing clothes into the washing machines, transferring the loads from one machine to another, or compressing the final products into baskets.

"If you took a movie film of it all, whichever way you ran it, forwards or backwards, it would look the same. I always imagined that they are making exacting preparations for that one special event that would colour their existences and make life worth all the bother. Needless to say the moment never comes, so the preparations continue and continue until frailty or death interferes with their ability to manipulate the machines."

With the morbid thoughts of the vendor in mind I walked through the back door to the garden. It was like stepping into a solid block of darkness.

Usually, however meagre, there is some source of illumination, the vendor's garden however was entirely devoid of any light.

"Well, what do you think of it? The unusual feature? What do you think of it?"

I realised if I craned my head right back and looked straight upwards I could see a narrow band of stars. Cutting up through the stars was a thin black triangle.

"Is it some form of church?"

My voice bounced straight back at me, indicating that I was inches away from a wall.

"No. Better than that. It's a mausoleum."

The vendor spoke with barely suppressed glee. I found it difficult to share his enthusiasm. My eyes became accustomed to the dark and I could just make out a row of hideous gargoyles leering down at me from above the entrance.

"They always say that today's luxuries are tomorrow's necessities. No home should be without one."

I found myself struggling for words.

"How? How did it get here?"

I shivered in the cold night air. I simply wanted to go home and not be subjected any more to the inevitable details.

"It was a stroke of luck really. Not many builders are capable of this sort of thing nowadays. They're all pre-cast concrete and asbestos tile. I had the good fortune to come across a builder by the name of Carp. Carp worked from basic stone. He was obviously well past his prime but apparently had the knowhow to tackle the job. We agreed on a remarkably modest price, shook hands and then I didn't see him again for several months. To be quite honest I'd given up hope, fearing all along that the project was doomed never to get off the ground. Then unexpectedly, without a hint of warning, one Monday morning Carp appeared in a rickety, black van with a solitary deficient aide. Once more my heart sank. I couldn't imagine this old man getting beyond the foundations before dropping dead. However, I had misjudged Carp. He was a wily old builder. With his mentally challenged aide, he removed from his van sections of corrugated iron and erected, in the front garden, a simple hut. The hut completed, he opened the door and out came a substantial group of workmen. They looked emaciated and grey as if they hadn't eaten, or breathed fresh air, for several months, their eyes blinking in the sunshine. Yet, despite their emaciation they were strong. You could see the tendons and muscles protruding from their arms as much as the ribs from their chests. They were obviously happy to work in what appeared from the outside to look like a brutal regime. They had great love for Carp and Carp had great love for them. The harder he made them work the more they loved him, the more they loved him the harder he made them work. The work progressed at an ever-increasing rate. They started the foundations in the autumn and had them finished by Christmas. The walls and pillars were completed by Easter and the vaulted ceiling by mid-summer. The whole thing was done within a year of starting. Throughout, I never saw the men eat anything apart from scraps thrown from Mr Carp's well-laden table, permanently situated at the edge of the building site. In the end, they were even thinner than when they started. On the other hand Mr Carp had substantially gained weight. Their mutual love had grown in proportion to Mr Carp's girth. The men limped back into the corrugated iron hut and Mr Carp, with his mentally challenged aide, collapsed the hut and packed the sections back into the van. Mr Carp drove off to his next job and I never saw him again. Shortly afterwards, he died in mysterious circumstances. He is now buried in an uncharacteristically modest grave in the churchyard in the village of his birth. A nice spot overlooking the sea, I believe.

"Well, that is how it got here. As I said, the price was extremely modest. It was substantially cut down from the original estimate on Mr Carp's suggestion that I file a bogus insurance claim. I'm surprised the estate agent didn't include a description of it in the brochure."

"But what is it for? I mean it can't be to store your ancestors because, in your case, they all seem to be alive."

"That's true. It isn't for my ancestors, it is for my son." He started to pat his pockets.

"I'm sorry. I seem to have left the key under the plant pot, by the front door. Don't tell me. I know it's silly and that I'm inviting burglars, but it's just a bad habit I've got into. I'll just pop and get it. I bet you're dying to see inside."

Not without some dread, I wondered what possibly could have been in there that would have been of interest to burglars.

The vendor opened the back door and started to disappear inside.

"I wonder where Fletcher has got to? If you happen to see him, maybe you could throw him a few sticks."

I was left alone in the darkness beside the mausoleum. Less than a minute had passed before I could hear heavy breathing. There was a brief pause and I tried to make out where it was coming from.

"Good dog."

Something charged at me with a vicious speed.

I started to run along the gravel path that surrounded the mausoleum.

Whatever was chasing me was deliberately maintaining my speed. A high fence had been placed the whole way round the mausoleum offering absolutely no means of escape. I passed the entrance.

As I ran round the second time my thoughts were peculiarly clear.

"Modern semi. Three up, two down. There must be a gap between the houses."

I came round again and noticed that there was a way out, but it was barred by a gate. I stopped to fiddle with the catch but I failed to open it in time and had to set off round the mausoleum a third time.

The next time round I planned to scale the gate. Unfortunately, when I reached it the dog was already there, waiting.

Ignoring the pains in my chest I turned round, I started to run back the way I'd just come. I felt something push me hard between my shoulders and I fell face down on the gravel, the tiny stones digging into my cheek.

I felt myself being carefully lifted up and placed on my back. Warm currents of moist air carrying the odour of raw meat wafted across my face.

My head was pushed back and a hot tongue gently touched me on the throat.

First, in saliva, a circle was drawn. A cross within the circle was then added. I closed my eyes tight as teeth began to raise a small cone of skin from the centre. The cone was pulled out until the skin was stretched tight. Gently it was extended further until the flesh between the teeth severed and I could feel a small quantity of blood trickle warm down my neck. The tongue mopped up the blood and sharp incisors started to probe inside the circumference of the tiny wound.

Suddenly my eyelids were penetrated by a glow of what seemed to be a beatific light. I opened my eyes and the silhouette of a saviour expanded rapidly from a point within the blinding globe before me.

"Jolly good. I see you've found Fletcher. I was just beginning to worry about him. He's certainly the life and soul of this place. He's obviously taken a liking to you."

The vendor was standing in the opening of the back door.

I sat up. Fletcher has disappeared.

Aching, I rose to my feet. There was a large tear in my trousers. I could feel that the knee was grazed but I couldn't make out how much of the stain beneath the tear was dirt or blood. I pressed my handkerchief against the wound on my throat.

The vendor was oblivious to my injuries. He was excitedly pushing the key into the lock of the mausoleum door.

The door swung open and I followed the vendor into the mausoleum.

"This has one or two luxury features that older mausoleums lack."

He indicated an electric light switch just beside the entrance.

"No problems seeing inside."

He threw the switch and a dingy, orange light came on some distance away. It hardly penetrated the darkness of the interior.

"I'm sorry it's not a little more illuminating. I had hoped for an impressive chandelier in addition to a plentiful supply of wall lights. However, Mr Carp was a mason not an electrician. He was only able to wire in one light bulb and switch. Still, you can't expect everything can you?"

His voice echoed off the walls.

We appeared to be making our way toward a large rectangular structure in the centre of the interior. The whole place had a musty, damp smell like the crypts in old churches.

"Yes. I'm sorry about that. If not for his death, I would have insisted that Carp come back to have a look at the damp-course."

As we approached the centre the echo from the vendor's voice was becoming more pronounced. I could see that, lying on top of the rectangular structure, was the figure of a small boy.

At first I thought it was the actual body of the vendor's child, but when we stood beside the casket I could see that it was an immaculate sepulchral carving.

My meagre knowledge of sepulchral carvings was that the figure represented the calm repose of the deceased in the sleep of death. This figure lay in contorted agony. Its fists were clenched and face was frozen in an endless scream.

Involuntarily I stepped backwards.

"It is a bit of a surprise, isn't it. I said my son was a plucky little chap and had only one fear. Unfortunately the fear was death itself. The only way to escape from his fear was by leaving through the exit that he dreaded most."

The echoes connected the vendor's words together into one confused mass. It was as if hundreds of birds had gathered to beat their wings on my head.

I started to walk away.

"I'm sorry but I'm the father of two small children. What do you really expect me to do in these circumstances. I can't possibly expose them to this."

For the first time the vendor was following me rather than the other way round.

I emerged from the interior into sharp, night air.

"Yes, I can see that possibly, yes possibly, some of the problems with this house may be solvable. But to expect us to live with the agony of your son, cast eternally in stone, is too much."

"Maybe you'd like to talk in terms of a price reduction then."

"I don't think so."

We passed between the houses.

"Your mind's made up."

"Yes."

Hastily we walked up the garden path.

"You've decided to move into the country then?"

"I don't know yet. I'll have to discuss it with my wife."

The gate was closed behind me. Although I didn't look round again I suspected that the vendor was leaning on it.

"If you change your mind about this house, or want to know any more details, it would be best to go through the estate agent."

"Thanks."

I was getting further away, my car was parked some distance up the street.

"Well anyway, I wish you all the best wherever you end up. I hope you find your Utopia and that it doesn't wind up like this place."

The vendor's voice got smaller and smaller until it vanished.

I parked the car in the drive of my house and looked through the windscreen. I could see the fractured images of my two children peeping through the distorting glass of the front door, as they waited to greet me.

As I locked the car door I wondered how presentable I was. I reached down and felt the tear on the knee of my trousers. My throat was still sticky with a mixture of blood and Fletcher's odorous saliva.

As I walked up to the house something rustled in the hedge.

I couldn't get rid of that awful feeling that something was watching me.

Anomie

When I entered the surgery Dr Twixt was scribbling something down.

'How can I help?'

It was one of those touchy matters that I didn't know where to start.

'Just take your time.'

Dr Twixt was doing the reassuring thing, but it wasn't particularly convincing. He was juggling a partially sucked matchstick in the right-hand corner of his mouth.

I hadn't taken Dr Twixt to be a smoker. I thought all GPs had given up smoking. Maybe he'd repented and the match sucking was all that was left of his bad habit.

Occasionally, as it wagged up and down, he almost lost control and it threatened to dislodge. To keep a grip of it he had to clench his teeth harder which forced him to exhibit a nauseating grin that could have been interpreted as supercilious. When even this measure failed to reconnect Dr Twixt with the matchstick, he was forced to take the red phosphorus bulb between finger and thumb and make a manual adjustment. Most times it was to slide the matchstick back a centimetre or so, but once or twice he had to prevent it going too far the other way. The latter occurrence was relatively rare, presumably because of the back-up provided by his tongue.

Certainly the tongue seemed to be working hard in the background, providing the muscle for the juggling act.

'The other day I was entering the supermarket. The automatic doors had opened for the people in front of me but when I was walking in they began to close.'

'And you were injured and hope to claim compensation from the supermarket?'

'No. I managed to slip through before they actually closed. But on the way out I went through different doors and this time they failed to open.'

'Maybe they were broken. Surely this is more a matter for an engineer rather than a physician.'

'I stood there for a minute or two looking helpless and trying to claw it open but as soon as somebody came up behind me they slid open.'

Dr Twixt remained relatively blank.

'Even the automatic doors of the surgery refused me admission. I had to attract the attention of the receptionist.'

Dr Twixt seemed to accept the seriousness of the situation.

'Is this a new symptom or have you experienced similar before?'

'It's gone on most of my life one way or another but it seems to be getting worse.'

'Do you notice that you fail to leave any memory trace in your encounters with people?'

'Pardon?'

'Do you find that people who you have encountered previously deny having met you?'

'Most of the time.'

'Most?'

'Well, all of the time. Most of my life. There were exceptions. My mother ...I think. To a degree.'

Dr Twixt swapped the matchstick from the right-hand corner to the left by a purely oral manoeuvre. I sensed diagnosis was about to be delivered.

'Sounds like chronic anomie.'

'What does that mean?'

'It is a common condition. Maybe in your case it is best characterised as a disassociation from the accepted values of society, possibly because of underlying lack of overall purpose in life. You simply present no obvious criterion for people to recognise you. Isolation in one form or another often breeds anomie which in turn reinforces isolation. It's the old vicious circle. You are gradually disappearing. The fact that you are no longer detected by impersonal electronic devices shows that your condition is deteriorating.'

'Is there a cure? Is it contagious?'

'In a sense it is catching. Not in the way that measles or influenza are spread by germs. It is more of a social phenomenon. Humans are simple, imitative creatures. Probably you contracted it from social intercourse with a friend or even from watching a character from a television soap opera. The condition is not usually considered to be fatal. But, if I'm to be completely honest with you, it is not known exactly what happens in the end. Ultimately does it count as death or non-death? Nobody knows for sure. Often people suffer from anomie but don't realise it. In cases less extreme than yours people continue to live relatively normal lives. They evade the condition by seeking pleasures and rewards of all kinds. There are a number of 'fixes' available. They indulge in the many varieties open to the consumer: drink, drugs, mescaline, caffeine and, ironically, consumerism itself, being the most notable. Many sufferers dutifully vote once every five years in the illusion they will one day acquire a caring, representative government that will put their predicament to rest. As well as 'external' fixes there are a number of 'internal' fixes. Probably these provide most of the coping mechanisms. Certainly there is no shortage of dopamine junkies, serotonin freaks and adrenalin addicts in the world. People crave recognition, careers, promotion, status, power, friendship. They opt for oodles of sex with a succession of partners. Sometimes they are trying to forget, sometimes they are trying to remember. They're even prepared to make babies in the hope that at least one of them might notice them, but by old age their hopes are invariably dashed. And, when all that fails, there's always religion and fast cars.'

The matchstick in Dr Twixt's mouth is really beginning to annoy me. I thought by now that it would have been chewed completely away. I'm beginning to see it as a spindly, wagging finger of accusation, bizarrely protruding from the mouth, bathed in spittle with a swollen end.

'Have you ever suffered from anomie, doctor?'

'A physician is structured by definition to shunt the sufferers of anomie through the manifold of disease. In order to provide an essential service as complex as this, the physician must be in a state of constant improvement and reinvention. This allows no time for anomie. Our chosen profession requires us to make constant modifications to our own physiologies. Within the physician's brain we have dramatically increased the transmission speeds along the neural networks to around 700 metres per second by replacing the myelin insulation of the axons with a synthetic material derived from advances in polymer research. In the future we are looking to speeds in excess of 1000 metres per second. In fact, almost twenty five percent of the neurons have been replaced by a variety of microscopic solid state devices installed by means of nanotechnology. Also we have replaced the iron-based haemoglobin with the copper-based hemocyanin. This allows us to perform successful diagnoses in much colder conditions and in environments with restricted oxygen such as underwater.'

'So your blood is blue now?'

'Yes. Very good. Well spotted. That is not to suggest at all that the physician has assumed aristocratic status, although interbreeding is no longer biologically possible. It also has various immunotherapeutic effects against a number of cancers. More recently we've been able to successfully replace the water in the blood stream with a volatile substance that I'm not allowed to reveal the name of but retains the necessary electrolytic properties of water. This has increased the speed and efficiency of the blood while reducing the risk of strokes and coronary thrombosis.'

'It sounds a bit of a fire hazard to me.'

Dr Twixt was full of joy and contempt at my response.

'That's exactly your problem. You see the world in terms of the negatives rather than attempting to build on the problems that arise. The doctors simply see this as a new challenge. For the first time in the history of the human form, we have installed fire-retarding properties by appropriately modifying our own DNA. We can no longer catch fire.'

'To cure myself do you think that I should become a doctor?'

Immediately I realised my mistake. The snort of contempt was going to be massive. By now I was really beginning to find Dr Twixt insufferable and the matchstick began to wag triumphantly in judgement over me. I suddenly noticed my disposable lighter, as I felt deep in my pocket. Yes, Dr Twixt, I am an unrepentant smoker. It was at this point of actually feeling the lighter in my hand that I suffered a catastrophic failure to repress a mischievous impulse to ignite the waggling matchstick.

I thought I would just give him a surprise.

It was certainly the case that he looked astonished as the lighter unexpectedly flared up in his face and the business end of the match burst into flames. Dr Twixt's astonishment lasted for about a second then, to my surprise, his head vanished in a solid blue flame that reached the ceiling. It really wasn't what I expected to happen. It came straight out of his neck, leaving him in a seated position with his clothes still pristine. A round patch on the ceiling started to glow orange. Quite quickly cracks formed and then pieces of plaster started to fall out leaving a hole. A distant gasp of astonishment from the room above issued from the hole, followed by the sound of a roaring flame.

I presumed that Dr Partridge had similarly ignited.

I had the strong impression that the other doctors in the building, by whatever mechanism, were going up like Roman candles.

Fire alarms quickly sounded and sprinklers started to efficiently distribute water around the room. It did little to quench Dr Twixt's fire. He continued to burn like an exotic firework but without the production of sulphurous smoke and with a minimum of ash. The flame remained clean and harsh.

I stood up and left the room.

There was chaos in the corridor as people were trying to escape. Police and firemen had arrived with astonishing speed and were already trying to impose order. I walked along the corridor with the surveillance cameras recording the scene as if collecting background footage for a disaster movie. But I was confident that I would show up as little more than an indistinguishable blur.

I was aware that the automatic doors wouldn't open for me but I knew that this wouldn't matter.

The antiterrorist squad were pouring into the building, conveniently keeping the door open for me. I slipped between them like a spectre, invisible in the daylight.

More police cars and ambulances were arriving in the car park.

I walked unseen through the middle of them.

I kept walking till the sounds of the sirens and alarms were replaced by pleasant birdsong.

Eva Von Crumhorn's Crumhorn

I'm trying to explain to Eva that women have remained silent in the world at large. Silent or invisible, I can't tell. Of course she can't hear me. Too busy in the kitchen preparing tea.

Eva?

No reply.

Eva Crumhorn?

Still no reply.

Eva Von Crumhorn?

That always gets her. There's no Von in the name.

'How many times must I say that there is no Von in my name.'

The vessel she uses to make tea is very unusual. Eva's explained it all to me. It is a crumhorn made of glass and rings a pure tone when the spout of the kettle bearing boiling water touches the rim. I can hear the boiling water draining into its depths to infuse the particular herbs of her choice. As it fills, the pitch alters in a perfect scale. I have the impression that it is capable of providing a sublime melody.

Eva, promised me that it is the herbs of healing.

Again, she doesn't reply.

It's herbs of healing that I require most.

I must explain that I am a dignitary from a distant planet.

Some time ago our sun swelled into a red giant. If that wasn't bad enough, the orbit of my world started to deteriorate. Each year we came a little closer to the sun and the land became hotter. I am a patriarch in my natural land and it grieves me to think of the blisters that formed on the flesh of my children. I can't be altogether sympathetic. They insisted on picking at the blisters and peeling off the inviting bubbles of skin. Of course the protective barrier of water drained away and left painful open sores, red as the sun. I tried to warn them. But, like the people on your world, they are simple creatures of compulsion.

Their crying was unbearable and I promised to find help. The infrastructure of our society had decayed following the spate of natural disasters so there were few means left to help my wailing children. So I set off in the one available spaceship and I arrived on your planet to appeal to your natural morality for help.

And would you provide help for my sorry world?

I received nothing. I was ignored.

The only exception was Eva Von Crumhorn who had possession of a health restoring tea and she was more than willing to share it with me.

I must point out that Eva Von Crumhorn has never really believed my story. As the kettle was boiling she came through from the kitchenette to torment me.

'So there was only one spaceship on your world?'

Yes.

'It could only seat one person?'

Yes.

'It was not possible to squeeze even one more person aboard?'

No.

'So, why was it you?'

Because I was the best qualified to undertake the trip. I was the only one with the diplomatic skills to negotiate with alien governments.

'And you failed miserably. Were the citizens of your planets pleased that it was you and you alone who was escaping?'

No. They were angry. There were riots.

'There was bloodshed?'

Yes.

'Why didn't you build more ships? Or at least hold a lottery?'

Is this tea ready yet?

'When you failed why didn't you return to your people to explain what had happened? You could have set off and looked for another world that might have helped you better than this one.'

I started to weep but probably not convincingly enough for Eva.

You know why I couldn't have set off in my spaceship. We have discussed it repeatedly.

'As I understand it, it was because of the difference between the atmospheric pressure of your world and mine.

On my world the pressure is much lower so your volume increased dramatically and you were unable to squeeze back through the door of your spaceship. Is that right?'

Yes. Must we keep talking about this?

'And for some reason not fully explained your gravity also increased rendering you unable to support your own weight.'

You know I can't walk. Since I arrived here I have been forced to propel myself about in this sodding bath chair. Look, is this tea ready yet? Indeed my volume and gravity did increase alarmingly when I stepped off my spaceship. With the volume thing it was a matter of pure physics kicking in. The Gas Laws to be precise. Hold the temperature of a fixed mass of gas constant, if you decrease the pressure the volume will increase. The pressure on your world is much less than mine. I simply inflated beyond my natural size like a balloon.

'But the temperature didn't remain constant did it? The temperature must have been considerably cooler here. Your world was heating up. That would have probably compensated for the increase of volume due to the lower pressure. You would end up exactly the same size on both worlds.'

Just bring me my tea, you cow. I want my tea.

'So, are you as petulant on your home planet as you are on this?'

It's only you that provokes me.

'There are no women on your planet?'

Plenty. But they know where they stand.

'I bet they don't. Don't you think, considering we come from different planets, that it is highly improbable that you and I speak the same language.'

We definitely don't.

Eva moves back to the kitchen to finish the tea making.

And we never will.

That gives me an opportunity to put my case without interruption. Eva does distort things to make them sound worse than they actually are.

I don't want you thinking that I'm just a big fat man, in a smoking cap, sitting in a bath chair, whining. It is true that I smoke heavily but that is to regulate the difference between the internal and external pressure. To stop smoking would be foolish and dangerous. Hashish is similarly effective. I also need to drink heavily. Alcohol that is, not tea (or rainwater, or vinegar, or any variety of juices). The reason for that again is physiological. Recently I've tended to piss out a lot of steam. Again this is to do with me having a much higher temperature due to the tragic heating of my home world. Only alcohol has the correct volatility to provide adequate cooling. Otherwise I would burn like a modest volcano leaving nothing more than a trace of ash and soot. Eva's herbal tea is something new for me. I haven't tried it yet. She says it will cure something or other but I'm not sure what exactly. Personally I'm sceptical. But I admit I need curing.

(I can hear Eva bringing the tea trolley. I must speed up).

The weight increase I do find more difficult to explain. I am a little heavy. I'm fairly sure I accidentally picked up a tiny speck of superdense matter on my way to your planet. It must have penetrated the hull of my spaceship and then pierced my skin as I attended the control panel. I hardly noticed it at the time. No doubt flapping my hand at it as if it was an annoying gnat that had sneaked aboard undetected. Most likely it was a fleck of matter from a Neutron Star, probably weighing up to half a ton. Every day I systematically search the endless folds of skin to try to spot the troublesome splinter that is weighting me to this bath chair. But so far my endeavour has proved fruitless. After a year (or is it two?) on your world, I'm not yet halfway through my task.

Eva's back with the trolley, rattling with cups and spoons.

'So, what did you do to make the sun glow red and the orbit of your planet to decay?'

Not again. I thought we'd finished with all that. Can't I just have my tea?

'You did something didn't you? It didn't just do it on its own. Was it one thing or many? Did you do it alone or did you have accomplices?'

You make it sound as if I was an arch villain committing a crime. It just happened didn't it? It was just one of those things.

'Did you do it alone or did you have accomplices?

At this point I tried ignoring her. None of this was her business anyway.

Pain entered my left ear and I let out a cry. I can't believe she'd given it a sharp twist.

'Don't ignore me. Did you do it alone or did you have accomplices.'

I had accomplices.

'But only you managed to escape in the end.'

Yes.

The special teapot that I mentioned is sitting on the trolley.

It is shaped like a crumhorn, only it's made of glass as I mentioned earlier. The tea, located in the u-bend, is dark but perfectly clear like......

'Urine?'

Eva smiles.

That is quite rare. Have I told you that Eva is almost beautiful? Her hair is dark but ends in a severe line where her neck meets her shoulders. I suppose her problem is that she doesn't present herself as a woman.

But she does wear a garter. I have seen it with my own eyes. She wears a garter high up on her thigh. Even Eva has her naughty moments.

I need a bed bath Eva. I stink.

'I can't argue with that. I think it's the only thing we truly agree on.'

Well? You could do that for me Eva. I would forgo the tea even. It would make me very happy.

'Tomorrow.'

It's been tomorrow for as long as I remember. I need it now Eva. What will people think of me?

'Nobody comes to see you. What does it matter if you stink of piss?'

It's not piss, Eva. It's the accumulations of a hard life. We respect that on my world.

'All the men smell of piss you mean.'

What have I done for you to hate me so much Eva? What have we done? You're a nurse. Give me a bed bath. If I say please. I liked it when you hurt me, Eva. When you tugged my ear. Maybe we could combine the two. Don't make me plead, Eva.

'Maybe tomorrow. If you manage to walk to the conservatory on your own.'

You know I can't do that.

'You mean I have to trundle you in your bath chair.'

Please be kind, Eva.

She wheels me into the conservatory that grows a variety of leafy things in pots. She situates me at the midpoint between a tree bearing grapefruit and a tree bearing lemons so that I can look out across the bay. Cyclists patrol the promenade. Some on tandems, others as solitary prowlers. Backwards and forwards. Up and down.

A big red sun hangs over the sea, reminiscent of the sun from my own world.

I hear the music as she pours the tea into a delicate china cup. An ancient funereal lament that reverberates in my ligaments.

'Milk?'

Does that mean you're going to kill me?

'Why do you think that?'

I know I'm not the first dignitary from my world to visit your planet. It has been noted often in our history. So often we've come in our spaceships to show friendship and kinship and never return.

'How do you think I'm going to kill you?'

Poison.

'Poison?'

In the milk.

'And where do you think the milk has come from?'

From your breast.

'Do you think the milk of the mother is always poison?'

Always. Why else have the men of your world declined? If it isn't in the mother's milk what is it in?

'You exaggerate.'

It's always in the mother's milk, Eva. It's a deadly selective poison that she feeds to her children. The girls thrive and the boys wither. The girls go on to motherhood and the boys succumb to a dwindling life expectancy. They start to perish with the firstborn and by the lastborn they are entombed.

She brings over the cup.

'See it's clear. There's no milk in it. You are quite safe.'

Despite my reservations I find myself gulping it down as if there was no time to spare.

Then immediately I'm back on my own world. It is spring. The sun is finite and yellow in the sky. The meadow turns green and fills with tall flowers and butterflies. My wife greets me at the gate and children stream from her skirts. She takes my hand and smiles. When I see that it is Eva Crumhorn I know that I'm dying.

Back in my bath chair Eva is mopping my brow.

I am dying.

'Yes.'

But how am I able to finish this memoir? Is it not paradoxical that I seem to be able to write my own death scene?

'Not if I write it for you.'

But you will not tell the truth.

'I guarantee that I will.'

And there, brethren, I faded from your world and mine for good.

Did I actually ever learn anything?

I think not.

Do I suffer embarrassment?

Most definitely I do.

The Pillar of Sodom

It may seem odd, but I cannot recall my father's penis.

Now he is dead, and the object of my ignorance has gone to the grave. I could ask my mother, but theirs was a long, bitter marriage that doesn't invite that sort of question. In fact any questions that it did invite received little response.

Cindy, my sister, apparently had knowledge of the matter due to an archaic rite of passage but refused to supply a description.

Even my good friend Jeremy must have caught a glimpse in the infinitesimal instance, demarked by a light being switched on and the final, indignant disappearance of my father through the door. Unfortunately I failed to make my inquiries about Daddy's prick at the time and now Jeremy has lost his memory.

Well, all I can say is the old fart's dead. I suppose it's regarded as a bit of a tragedy when somebody dies leaving essential questions unanswered. However, it must be regarded as an act of utter, utter incompetence if, in addition to the matter of unanswered questions, I, the bereaved, may have been responsible for the death.

My father just wasn't that sort of father. On those bright, cold days that constituted my early childhood, when we were out in town and walking on hard frost with our bladders full, he wasn't the sort of father that instructed his son on the practical applications of the public urinal by method of example. Oh yes, we would patter down the concrete steps together into the acrid vault beneath the statues of heroes. But there, among the dripping cisterns, we would part company. I would be situated protesting before the urinal and he would vanish into a cubicle, slamming the door. I was deprived of all sightings of the paternal tool.

It's too easy to put it down to modesty or shyness. Personally I always thought it was due to status. He couldn't bear to pee with the rank and file. I have to assume that that included me.

He certainly had the credentials. There was the distinguished accent of the intellectual. I can't really imagine the true intellectual without the mid-European accent. One might think of Bohr, Brouwer or my father's fellow Polander, Tarski. He was constantly pointing out that when he was a student at Warsaw University between the wars, Tarski was professor of mathematics.

Who the hell is Tarski anyway?

Certainly the latter's 'Logic, Semantics and Metamathematics' was part of my father's vast library. It was a constant source of irritation to me that the ancient, puckered asshole that fathered me had been a distinguished scholar. He straddled languages and science and became a translator of scientific papers. He was the one that gave Feynman to the countries behind the Iron Curtain.

I can't deny that he was impressive. Although not a luminary in his own right, his work required him to be an adept practitioner of the mathematical arts. With nothing more than pencil and a piece of paper he could produce key-path integrals somewhat like a good musician produces Bach from a simple pipe.

It's hard to imagine a man like my father not living a fascinating life. Living in Poland before the war. Living in Poland during the war. Living in Poland after the war. Living under Hitler. Living under the Communists. Living behind the Iron Curtain. He was a purpose built dissident whose mouth constantly issued moral analysis in an intricate, unfathomable language. I don't know how he'd have coped without brutal totalitarian regimes to feed his indignations.

Penultimately he ended up living in Doncaster. I can't exactly remember how he ended up in Doncaster but the story of his escape from Poland was sure to have been a fascinating one. He was the sort of person that, put down anywhere, in just his knickers and garters, would make out. In Doncaster he married my mother and, well in his fifties, fathered two children. I think this was less due to a longing for fatherhood than an exercise to demonstrate the steely wire of his erectile tissue and the potency of his seed.

It certainly impressed me. For a long time, in my misinformed youth, I believed those of an intellectual disposition suffered a chronic complaint of wasting genitalia. The extra blood supply demanded by their brains during their constant mental activities must have grossly impaired the

means of achieving even a half-decent stiffy. You might say
that my existence on this morbidly inclined planet was a
source of constant astonishment. In many ways he looked so
old and frail. I always noticed that his arse failed to fill his
trousers properly. The material sagged as if he was composed
of brittle spindles and pulleys. When he climbed in and out of
taxis with the aid of an umbrella, I always expected his
pathetic little legs to completely shear a short distance below
the knees.

Needless to say, I was extremely mistaken. As was
hinted by Papa himself, when Schrödinger wrote the equation
that bears his name, the lecherous physicist was enjoying a
dirty weekend with his mistress in the Swiss Alps.

My thesis of wasting genitalia was obviously mistaken.
I then began to notice that my father's library was swollen
with books possessing other than a mathematical nature.
There was an explicit book of Hindu pornography taken from
exquisite, colourful paintings. Little Indian gentlemen
performed acts of cunnilingus upon little Indian ladies. There
was a book of Victorian pornography. This strangely
resembled the Indian book, except that it contained black and
white photographs of whiskered Victorian gentlemen
performing acts of cunnilingus on Victorian ladies. There was
an unexpurgated 'Lady Chatterley, predating the trial. There
were several 'de Sades' and 'Henry Millers', in French, again
dating from the time when they were banned in this country.

My view of Daddy began to alter. I began to notice
that he actually looked like Henry Miller himself. A bald,

wizened, grinning Mandarin possessing more dimensions than I'd originally imagined.

From then on it was all different. The equations took on new interpretations. I could see my father seizing the consumptive Lawrence by the throat and taking him to task over the myth of simultaneous orgasms during sexual intercourse. I imagined my father, in haughty manner, pressing the wheezing writer's nose against a blackboard of formulas proving the incommutability of the operators of momentum and position.

I could hear him shouting.

'See, if the position of an electron is measured with total accuracy then it leaves the momentum completely undetermined. By direct correspondence we can infer that if the male orgasm is realised, the female orgasm is totally unachievable. If the female orgasm is realised it leaves the male orgasm unachievable......'

So much for history. When he was bored of parenthood he left my mother, my sister, myself and Doncaster for a short-lived fling with a much younger woman who still had dreams of completing a PhD. The next we heard he was living in France. Although well over the age of retirement, his skills as a translator and fornicator were apparently still in demand.

There were yet more revelations about Pater's sexual extravagances still to be revealed. For some time I was aware that Cindy had stopped seeing our father, I assumed that it was due to natural lapse. Again, I was completely mistaken.

I received from father a letter. Characteristically it was constructed pretentiously in Joycean flow and was thus virtually unreadable.

> *dear kth product of the sweetmusic of*
> *the joystring of cocks*
> *i am soon to your door when my*
> *journey bled and done. i still pray as*
> *if it were a god that you fitted fine*
> *another with warmcocks and tongues*
> *and promises #dddy worries# for the*
> *space surrounding notfor*
> *sisters&daughter&wives but for*
> *empty space*

Painfully, I attempted translation and came to the fairly certain conclusion that he was making a brief visit to Britain and was requesting an audience. The last bit I wasn't too sure about. He may have been lamenting my current lack of life-partner and establishing that he cared not about my sexual orientation. I also wondered if he was alluding to the absence of Cindy in his life.

Cindy lived a short distance from my own squalid abode in the Midlands. We met at a mutually acceptable point and I asked her. She had taken to smoking roll-ups and wearing black, like a goth. Her eyes were now extravagantly painted and her beautiful long hair was dyed black, shorn and upright. In Bank's coffee shop I pushed my fingers through her hair and watched the waves move like a breeze through a cornfield. She seemed irritated by my interference at the same time as putting her head forward as if she was enjoying the sensation. I think she was trying to tell me that our father had strange beliefs but I didn't quite know where it was going.

She stopped.

I tried to assist.

'Yes, I know. He insists that I'm homosexual. In fact ever since I was five he has insisted that I'm a homosexual.'

As I became aware that I was rambling I also became aware that my effort to assist was redundant and obstructive. Cindy paused and then began again.

'He has many strange beliefs and one of them is that it is up to the father to initiate his daughter in sexual practices.'

'No.'

I admitted some disgust at the suggestion, to mask my fascination. Suddenly the implication occurred to me in full.

'He didn't though, did he? I mean, he might suggest it but it's a different matter to actually do it. Isn't it?'

'I don't want to discuss it further and I'm not going to see Father next week. In fact I'm not going to see him again.'

All this was a bit of a shock. I'm ashamed to say that I couldn't fully concentrate on what she said. I am aware of how shocking it was. But as she made the revelation, all that popped into my head was a thought about Papa's penis. It produced a memory of a photo from one of Father's books of the writer Henry Miller. Miller was in the nude on some Greek island with his mucker Lawrence Durrell. Since I'd already equated the appearance of my father with Henry Miller, it suddenly became obvious to work by analogy and assume similarity of penises. I remember Miller's prick as a long, heavy, drooping coil as if a naughty schoolboy had fashioned it out of soft clay. It wasn't that I doubted Miller's fabled virility but it seemed hard to imagine it achieving anything like an erection unless it was provided support by gears and pulleys powered by a small nuclear power station.

This shows what a poor brother I was. Any authentic brother by now would have skewered him from scalp to prostate and roasted him like a kebab on a naked flame. Yet I imagined he would be too scrawny and wizened to produce the required juices to decently baste him. His flesh would be cracked and desiccated. I would need a different approach.

The following week I travelled by train to London and met my father at Victoria Station. Although I hadn't seen him for some time he looked exactly the same. Small, intellectual, bespectacled, self-important with a furled umbrella, Macintosh and trilby. Anaemic and shrivelled.

We had lunch in a convenient tavern and we went through the usual agenda: When was I going to get a job? When was I going to become more like him? And when we reached our usual impasse, he asked if there was a point at which he would see Cindy.

'I mentioned your visit to Cindy. She was unable to make any commitment but mentioned something about paternal involvement in an initiation in some rite of passage.'

My father reacted not well.

'I see, so having heard one side of the situation you are now going to daub me with moral contours and proceed to dissect me along them?'

As he got uppity, I could imagine him going into full intellectual tirade. Axiom. Proposition. Proof. Lemma. Proof. Corollary. Proof. Theorem. Proof. Then the forearm smash, no doubt utilising Tarski's celebrated Truth Conditional thus demolishing me entirely.

'p' is true if and only if p

I circumvented this possibility.

'I don't mean that at all. It's more that I felt neglected. You always said that you thought I was homosexual. But if it is the role of the father to initiate his daughter in sexual practices, then if the son is homosexual, shouldn't it be the role of the father to initiate him also in sexual practices?'

'Don't be absurd. I'm sure you were initiated into sexual practices long before the age of consent. Anyway, Cindy needed help.'

'I suffer from chronic shyness as well.'

'Besides, the father would have to be homosexual as well, wouldn't he?'

'But obviously, with Cindy, the whole thing was a moral matter and you would have derived no direct personal pleasure from the act. It was simply a rational intervention. Anyway, I thought it was one of your boasts on those walking holidays in the Swiss Alps when you were younger.'

I certainly remember the black and white photographs of young me in obscene shorts making suggestive gestures with items of luggage. I could have made a mistake at this point. But I also have a feeling that there were goings-on in a sordid tenement in Cairo. This was told to me by my mother, but I think that was the occasion he contracted an unpleasant disease and became the first person to be successfully treated with penicillin for that particular complaint.

I didn't feel I was getting through so I made the plunge.

I swiftly pressed my hand high on his thigh and started to weep.

'Please Daddy. Please. Just once. Daddy. Please Daddy, you must help me.'

And there it happened. I assumed I was reaching for the dead but in reality touched the quick. From deep within his trouser I could hear a definite creak. The leathery prostate whispered 'Yes' and the shrunken testicles regained buoyancy. The penis, invisible to me all these years, bobbed with sheer joy.

He sat back, his throat moving visibly, like a pump to the fluids that were gathering unchecked in his mouth. His voice sounded different.

'I'll have to think about this. I must say it's a bit of a surprise. I don't know what to make of it. You'll have to wait. I'll telephone next week.'

We departed but I didn't have to wait long for his call. To my astonishment he accepted the strange offer two days later. There was a minor dispute as to where the event should take place, whether it should be the Swiss Alps, a tenement in

Cairo or just my hovel in Coventry. I got him to agree, slightly reluctantly, to the latter but first we would dine in a restaurant of his choosing.

I thought the best in the area was the Macdonald's but typically my father sniffed out a Polish restaurant. I really had no idea that there was a Polish restaurant within two hundred miles, let alone a few minutes' walk from my dwelling, but of course my father targeted it with characteristic speed and accuracy.

We pondered the menu. Personally I would have preferred burger and chips but in the end opted for pierogi. My father went all the way with pickled herring. As he spoke enthusiastically about the significance of various recurring symbols in mathematics and ancient mythology, I was engulfed in a briny wind that seemed to originate from an ocean afloat with the decayed bodies of seamen, dead fish and rotting seaweed.

We trotted back through the streets suitably charged with Zubrowka. I felt just a little bit nervous. Before being in the restaurant with him I'd never been so close to him as to smell his breath before. It had never particularly occurred to me that he actually breathed. Now that we were on our way home I was conscious of his respiration. Maybe it was the excitement, but he mainly breathed through his mouth as if he was making an obscene phone call.

I unlocked the door admitting us to the blackness of my flat. My father reached out to switch the light on but I put out my hand to restrain him.

'I'm sorry, I don't think I can manage with the light on.'

He seemed almost caring and gentle. I'd always thought of him as a combatant but now he was the embodiment of consideration.

I heard him undressing in the dark and was aware of his movements in the dark against the crack of hall light through the edge of the door. Finally there was the unromantic twanging of the sprung mattress as he climbed into the bed. With two bodies in the bed now, it creaked like an old sailing ship tossing on a stormy ocean in search of a new land.

I think I hardly need to point out that it wasn't actually me up there on the top of the bed exchanging pleasures with my father. Despite the strong belief of my father, to be quite honest, I'm not that way inclined. Fortunately my good friend Jeremy is, and he was more than willing to act as a substitute. In the duration, I was beneath the bed, at some times in fear of my life in case the springs sheared and the two bodies came crashing down on me and caused me serious injury. With the violence of the rocking motion, tiny particles of dust from the underside of the mattress dropped into my eyes causing them to smart and blink continuously.

Finally it all came to one final climax and the movement above stopped.

It all went very quiet.

My father began a typical analysis of the whole thing but the wrong voice answered him. The lamp beside the bed was switched on and the specs went on. An angry, indignant voice started up. Thin, sinewy legs came over the bedside and dangled into my view. Hastily, trousers were dragged up them and the feet were plunged into socks and shoes. Within seconds he was fully dressed, had gathered up his hat and umbrella and was marching out of the room. He turned briefly, without speaking, to view Jeremy reclining on the bed and me poking out from beneath like an unwelcome rodent, then he walked out. This was my last view of him.

I thought this showed thoroughly bad manners and a poor sense of humour. Jeremy had done his best to please him and there wasn't even a hint of a thank you. I thought at least there might be a bit of post-penetrative conversation such as.

'How was it for you?' or 'My ignorant son doesn't know what he's missing' or even 'That was very nice Jeremy, but why do you look so gaunt and wasted. I hope you are not sickening for something.'

My father died a couple of years later and his ashes were scattered near the small town where he was born. I am ignorant of the cause of his death. He may have fallen down the stairs or suffered a stroke. Of course I always prefer to think that his death was related to my little joke, thoughtfully situated in a time before state of the art medicine made elastic the duration of sufferer's lives.

Jeremy is also unable to provide information on this matter or any other. Not even the smallest revelation regarding the disposition of father's penis. Sadly Jeremy's eyes have now developed the dry, uncomprehending glisten of boiled sweets.

The Proof of Miracles

Division

My most distinct memory of Bartholomew is of him wearing his new khaki shorts for the summer. The effect was only slightly marred by the presence of his knickers drooping from one of the trouser legs.

We were waiting for Mrs Pugh. Bartholomew had had one of his ideas and was eager to try it out. He knew at this time of the morning she would be out shopping and would return soon. We occupied the idle moments by playing trains in the succession of neighbours' gardens.

Mrs Pugh appeared at the end of the street on her bicycle.

The moment was approaching and Bartholomew was ready.

'Good Morning Mrs Poo.'

Mrs Pugh failed to notice the mispronunciation of her name. Her bicycle was approaching the perigee of its trajectory.

'Good Morning Bartholomew. You are a nice, polite little boy today. Wait till I tell your Mummy what a nice polite little boy you are now.'

The bicycle started to draw away. I wondered if Bartholomew's little scheme going to fail.

'Good Morning Mrs Poo.'

She was still smiling.

'No, Good Morning Mrs Poo. Mrs POO. POO. POOOO.'

Mrs Pugh turned round on the saddle. The bicycle teetered.

'You are a rude boy Bartholomew. Wait till I tell your Mummy what a rude little boy you really are.'

Bartholomew sniggered into his hand.

She couldn't tell Mummy what a rude little boy he was.

There was no way she could possibly achieve this, because Mummy was dead.

I had been aware for some time that Bartholomew was planning the perfect crime.

Perfection, in Bartholomew's sense of the term, did not refer to the careful attention to the details that would ensure that the identity of the perpetrator of a crime remained permanently hidden. Instead, Bartholomew was more concerned with symmetry, precision, form and, most importantly, sound metaphorical interpretation of the event.

At the peak of his tantrums and moments when he was being unreasonably demanding, Bartholomew carefully monitored Mummy's responses.

'There aren't two of me Bartholomew.'

'I can't be in two places at the same time Bartholomew.'

'You can't expect me to tear myself in two for you Bartholomew.'

Inspired, Bartholomew began to consider solutions to Mummy's dilemma.

He fashioned a homuncule from plasticine.

Then, taking the carving knife from the kitchen drawer, he carefully spliced it along the transverse plane. The upper and lower halves fell apart.

Bartholomew examined the result.

He realised the symmetry between the arms and legs was poor. There was no sufficient duplication of head and neck on the lower part of the body.

Bartholomew was forced to reject this division as a solution to Mummy's dilemma. He rejoined the two parts of the homuncule.

He contemplated division along the coronal plane.

The asymmetry between the front and the back was obvious without making the cut.

This left only one reasonable solution to Mummy's dilemma.

Bartholomew would have to dissect her along the median plane.

It was only recently that he'd found cause to condemn his father to fire. I recall the discussion that led to this conclusion.

'So, Mummy, let's get this straight. Every morning when I wake up in my little cot, Daddy has already left for work?'

'That's right Sweetheart.'

'Every night when he returns, it invariably occurs at a time when I'm back in the old cot and have been long asleep?'

'That's right Sweetheart.'

'When I awake in the small hours of the morning with one of my frequent nightmares and have to sleep in your bed, it always seems that Daddy has also had one of his attacks of insomnia and is downstairs making a cup of tea or is raiding the refrigerator. Is that correct?'

'That's right Sweetheart.'

'He works weekends and bank holidays.'

'Yes sweetheart.'

'From humanitarian concern he spends each Christmas with his chronically ailing mother.'

'Yes sweetheart.'

'It seems to me that Daddy, by definition, occupies a space permanently separated from the space I occupy.'

'It might appear a bit like that Sweetheart.'

'Is it not a little sinister that the space Daddy occupies always lies beyond any means of sensory communication?'

'Try not to look at it like that sweetheart.'

'So, despite Daddy's apparent invisibility, he remains a being of infinite moral rectitude. If I'm being naughty, and/or practising my empirical investigations, then I'm posed with the threat of not being allowed to form what appears to be a mystical union with my father in some ethereal theme park located in the abstraction of the adult imagination.

'Let me put it like this Mummy. Does your notion of Daddy contain any abstract reasoning concerning quantity or number? No. Does your notion of Daddy contain any experimental reasoning concerning matter of fact and existence? No. Then commit him to the flames Mummy, commit him to the flames, for he is nothing but sophistry and illusion.'

So, in a sense, Daddy was relegated to a few discarded ashes.

Mummy fared little better.

From Bartholomew's activities earlier that morning, Mummy had come to resemble identical twins, floating sideways, in parallel, in the placid ocean of the linoleum on the kitchen floor.

I felt sure Bartholomew, eventually, would begin to miss Mummy. Probably Daddy too, even if only as a means of reasonable moral restraint.

'Yes I'm sure you're right to some extent. But, at the same time, I have to point out that the limits of my domain, at least up till now, extended little further than the nursery. These restraints were beginning to impose a serious threat to my development. In the interests of natural growth, for better or worse, Mummy and Daddy had to go.

'For example, the unnecessary rationing of tasks for breakfast is now lifted. I have free access to the refrigerator. I may use the drinks cabinet as often as I wish and can have a cigarette occasionally which, incidentally, both having been denied to me in what I consider to be acts of spiteful hypocrisy. I am now going to celebrate by having a gin and tonic and a smoke, and then I'm going out to catch Mrs Pugh as she comes in from her shopping. I've been meaning to be rude to her for some time but couldn't face the consequences.'

I watched Bartholomew recline on the settee with dirty shoes up on the cushions, one hand clutching his drink, the other supporting his head.

This all seemed quite an achievement for someone not quite four years old. His birthday was tomorrow.

As he expelled smoke through his nostrils he became subdued and pensive.

'I was disappointed with my division of Mummy. I meant it to be symmetrical, but when I was actually performing it I discovered there were all manner of internal organs that I hadn't anticipated. The fault lay in the inadequacy of the plasticine model, it assumed a quality of homogeneity where there was none. The symmetry was ruined. I must remember not to use plasticine again in forward planning.'

Unity

The abuse of Mrs Pugh successfully completed, we re-entered the house by the front door. I asked Bartholomew what his next plan was.

'Call it a mission. I feel it is far more appropriate to refer to this as a mission.'

He leaned against the rocking horse in the nursery, playing with the box of matches.

'In this odd little world of ours, I have long been troubled by the divisions that fragment what could be an exquisite unity. In the house to the left of us, we have Wilberforce, in the house to the right, we have Scarratt. How can we be expected to tolerate divisions such as these?'

I wondered if he was simply referring to the problems that arose from the differences in their relative sizes. Scarratt was bigger and older than Bartholomew, and took advantage of the brutal possibilities that this difference offered. Wilberforce was younger and smaller, but Mummy had always denied Bartholomew the pleasure of acting likewise.

Bartholomew seemed annoyed at this suggestion.

'No, no, no, no, no. You don't understand. I'm not talking about petty squabbling and revenge. I'm talking about the achievement of peace and prosperity through the subtle application of reason. Consider Wilberforce, with his inane nursery rhymes and his collection of pressed wild flowers. You see him entering woodland thick with bluebells and what does he do? He picks one, one sodding bluebell. Why? To conserve the wildlife. Why? Why? Why shouldn't he pick as many as he wants? He needs help. He needs me to re-educate him. He must be taught not to live in the poverty of self-denial. He must learn to devour whole fields of wild flowers if he wishes.'

I wondered what Bartholomew intended for Scarratt.

'Scarratt? Oh, he's just an animal. He can choose between social elevation or remaining, trapped forever, in his squalid burrow.'

Bartholomew shook the box of matches.

'The tools for the completion of these little tasks are fire and void.'

We went into the back garden.

Immediately we heard the tuneless, high-pitched intonation of a little boy singing.

'I listen to the larks,

singing up on high.

Tra-la, tra-la, tra-la.

Within the blue canopy,

We like to call the sky.

Tra-la, tra-la, tra-la.'

Bartholomew entered the next door garden through a hole in the fence. Wilberforce was leafing through the volumes of pressed flowers while sitting in the middle of the lawn.

'Like a busy bee,

within the hive.

Tra-la, tra-la, tra-la,

I think how lucky I am,

To be alive.

Tra-la, tra-la ---------.'

'Hello Wilberforce, that's a pretty little song. Did you make that up all on your own? It certainly expresses a sentiment I endorse.'

A slight smirk momentarily formed in one corner of Bartholomew's mouth.

'Oh, hello Bartholomew. I composed it only this morning actually. Anyway, what are you doing here? I know your Mummy's banned you from coming here again, because you bully me.'

'Well. Let's say she's had a change of heart. She's equipped me with the tools of fire and void to bring about a unity between you, me and Scarratt.'

'I'm playing no part in this. If it means you're going to pretend to be my friend and then continue to be nasty to me, then I'm just not interested. Or if you think just because Scarratt is bigger and stronger than you, that I'm going to take your side in this silly war you're both waging in the hopes that it might increase your chance of winning, then you're mistaken. And as to being equipped with the tools of fire and void, I haven't the faintest idea what you are talking about.'

Bartholomew took the matches from his pocket. Wilberforce looked shocked.

'I'm sure your Mummy doesn't let you play with those.'

'More than that, I have full access to the drinks cabinet now.'

Bartholomew struck a match.

'See the possibilities of the fire as it consumes the matchstick.'

'Stop it, you're being silly. If you're not careful you're going to set something on fire.'

Suddenly the first page of Wilberforce's book of pressed wild flowers was curling up, the flame almost invisible in the bright sunshine.

Wilberforce screamed.

'Stop it. Stop it. Stop it.'

'This really is a testimonial to your ability to press and dry flowers. See how well they burn. Aren't the little sparks coming off the leaves of the purple milk-vetch fascinating to watch?'

Wilberforce was wailing like a mourner at a funeral pyre.

'Right, what have we next? Sweet violet? Meadow saxifrage? Or what about this rather splendid display of rare orchids?'

'I'm going to tell my Mummy.'

'Well, of course you can do that, but by the time she comes this whole collection of pressed wild flowers will be little more than the covers that bind it.'

Wilberforce's mouth dropped open.

Bartholomew was sitting, gazing through the window.

'I think we can count on Wilberforce's cooperation now.'

I could see Wilberforce, busy, in Scarratt's garden. He had climbed the tree at the end, and was smashing up Scarratt's tree house with an axe.

'Having been given the appropriate stimulus, he appears to show boundless energy in any task I set him.'

Because Scarratt was a little older, he had just started school and wouldn't be back till after four o'clock.

Bartholomew was pleased with the progress.

'I think everything will be ready in time.'

When Scarratt arrived home, the three of us were carefully situated in Bartholomew's garden, pretending to be playing a game of cowboys and Indians.

He discovered the ruins of his tree house.

'Who's done this? Do you know anything about this Bartholomew?'

Bartholomew shook his head.

'Not me Scarratt. Maybe whoever did it left a note.'

Sure enough there was a large piece of paper pinned to the tree, covered with a scrawl of crayon.

> I HATE SCARRATT
> BECAUSE SCARRATT IS A BASTARD
> SIGNED
> SCARRATT

Bartholomew looked concerned.

'It appears to be an act of self-hatred Scarratt. An interesting variation of the theme of self-mutilation.'

'You've done this Bartholomew. You're dead.'

Scarratt leapt over the fence and charged towards Bartholomew.

He failed to notice a covering of fresh leaves situated just before Bartholomew's feet.

The leaves parted and Scarratt disappeared into the earth.

Bartholomew peered into the hole.

'Oh, there you are Scarratt. I wondered where you'd gone. Typical, all bluff and bluster. One minute pretending to be preparing for the kill, the next skulking in your burrow. I always said you were an animal, didn't I?'

Bartholomew accurately placed a globule of saliva in the middle of Scarratt's upturned forehead with the manner of an evangelist blessing a potential convert. He carefully chose his words.

'This is probably the greatest opportunity that you are likely to have in your lifetime, for personal development. I am going to offer you the possibility of ADVANCEMENT. You, Scarratt, may soon be making your first tentative steps towards becoming a HUMAN BEING. You may look forward to shedding your prehensile tail. I can say to you, 'Scarratt, stand up and walk towards me. Walk towards me on your HIND LEGS.' What do you say Scarratt?'

'Piss off.'

'I can wean you off these guttural utterances. Place your education in my hands, Scarratt. We can work together. Simply for the small price of obedience, I can transform your whole existence. Make me your mentor, and in my service, you can achieve limitless wealth and happiness. Are you with me, Scarratt?'

'Piss off.'

Scarratt made a huge leap upwards and just managed to catch hold of Bartholomew's foot. Bartholomew fell on to his back and, with arms helplessly flailing, he started to slide towards the hole.

'Quick Wilberforce.'

Wilberforce didn't look very enthusiastic.

'Burnet-saxifrage, purple-loosestrife, procumbent pearlwort, you berk.

Wilberforce jumped to life. Just as Bartholomew was rolling over the lip he managed to pull him back.

'You shit, Scarratt.' I'll make sure that you regret refusing my charity.'

In a frenzy, he started kicking at the earth around the edge of the hole.

'Get the wheelbarrow of soil.'

Wilberforce was too shocked at the suggestion to respond.

'Oh never mind, in the end I have to do everything.'

Earth began to fall over Scarratt.

'When I get out of here you're in trouble Bartholomew.

The earth continued to cover legs, abdomen, thorax, shoulders, neck and head. All the time Scarratt was intoning,

'When I get out of here you're in trouble, Bartholomew.'

'When I get out of here you're in trouble, Bartholomew.'

The voice turned into a frantic screech.

'Bartholomew.'

'Bartholomew.'

'Bartholomew.'

'Bartholomew.'

The only sign left of Scarratt was a writhing claw and a clump of brown hair matted with soil. The intonation became indistinguishable from a grunt, as the hole disappeared with the final barrowful of earth.

'Bartholom.'

'Bartholom.'

'Barthol.'

'Barthol.'

'Barth.'

'Barth.'

'Barth.'

Bartholomew wiped his hand on his tee-shirt.

'Witness the sad deterioration of language under duress. It sounds like nothing more than the distant barking of a dog. I always said that Scarratt was an animal.

Motive and Quest

Bartholomew dismissed Wilberforce. In dejection and misery, he went home.

With the collection of wild flowers still tucked under his arm. Bartholomew brushed the soil from his grubby shorts.

I began to think there was more to the matter than met the eye.

It seemed to me rather odd of Bartholomew to 'remove' Mummy just before his birthday.

'No. No. The presents were bought weeks ago and hidden in the accustomed secret place, i.e. the bottom of the wardrobe. The principle present was a tricycle. I've been using it for some time, in conjunction with some of the results of my empirical investigations. I might add the results have been spectacular. Also, most of the birthday tea party has been bought in. Not of course the crappy salmon paste sandwiches which we all have to endure in varying states of misery, but the good stuff like crisps, peanuts and, of course, the birthday cake decorated with four decent sized candles.'

But what about Scarratt? Didn't he have an understanding, so to speak, with Mrs Pugh's daughter, Constantine?

'He might have done.'

Didn't you, Bartholomew, rather fancy Constantine yourself?

'Well ...'

This concern for unity and peace was just a cover to achieve your desires?

'Well ...'

When you buried Scarrat, were you not simply burying the opposition?

'Well ...'

With Scarratt out of the way, you believe the way to Constantine's heart is open.

'O.K. O.K. There is some truth in what you say. In fact there is a lot of truth in what you say. However, you cannot appreciate the motive until a certain phenomenon is revealed, along with some of the results of my empirical investigations. I cannot show you here. We must go inside.'

We went into the cool of the house, stepping over two halves of Mummy in the kitchen.

I was certain that one half of Mummy winked at me. Bartholomew was too involved with his own activities to notice. I tried to mention it to Bartholomew, but he didn't seem able to listen.

Bartholomew drew the curtains.

'Prepare yourself for a surprise.'

He unbuttoned his trousers.

There in the shadows a serpent stirred in a nest of black hair.

'Do you have any recognition of this?'

It looks like an adult penis.

'Yes. Yes. But have you any idea what it can do? Its potential exceeds my wildest dreams. Mummy was shocked by my experimentation to such an extent that she had imposed prohibition. I could not allow that. The matters of fact arising from this thing were too important.

'For instance when I pictured Constantine in my head I couldn't help noticing the thing rising like my toy missile on its launcher. In the spirit of the true empiricist I observed the constant conjunction of thoughts regarding Constantine and the display of erectile properties. I was forced to the conclusion that the two events were causally related.

'There is more to the matter. There remains the property of the DETONATION.

'The DETONATION is proof that, underlying existence, is a principle of perfection. You see, I discovered at a certain point, when the mental images of Constantine started to flash faster and faster in my mind, the images fused into one sensation. A sensation of pure pleasure. At this instance, THE MISSILE, so to speak, DETONATED.

'When THE MISSILE detonated, a jet of fluid ejected across the room in a distinct arc. Not just a random squirt. Not a messy, dribbly spitting. It was a distinct arc. A perfect parabola.

'Needless to say I was anxious to repeat my experiment. I looked down to find the MISSILE was no longer there. Instead there was only a tiny, shrimp-like creature hiding in the thicket. You can imagine my surprise. I almost wondered if I had dreamed the incident. Then I spied the carpet and the 'Winnie the Pooh' wallpaper. There was a trail of soapy liquid across the floor and halfway up the wall.

'I awaited the return of the MISSILE. I wasn't disappointed. I practised over and over again. I DETONATED through a variety of angles. I DETONATED across Cartesian axes. I DETONATED over conic sections.

'My first impression was correct, the trajectory was a parabola. Utilising the mathematical techniques of the calculus of variations I demonstrated that the underlying principle was indeed a PRINCIPLE OF PERFECTION. The seeming arbitrary conjunction of Constantine, THE MISSILE and THE DETONATION led to a unity of pleasure and perfection. I began to realise the whole purpose of the enterprise of science was to reveal that unity.

'So you see, both Mummy and Scarratt were obstacles that had to be dealt with. Mummy had taken against THE MISSILE and especially THE DETONATION. So Mummy had to go. It is inevitable that Scarrat will get in the way of matters concerning Constantine. Going by the principle of perfection, it is obvious that Constantine is going to have an 'inverse complement' to my MISSILE. This has to be carefully investigated. Scarratt was clearly inadequate to this task. Despite being a roughneck, Scarratt had the physical credentials of a Cherub. With Scarratt out of the way my deadline for this particularly important investigation is tomorrow – Saturday – the day of my birthday. In order to prepare for this, we must check out the tricycle.'

He began to pull up his trousers.

'Bugger. I can always undo trouser buttons, but I can never manage to do them up again.'

We went into Mummy's bedroom.

Bartholomew opened the wardrobe and pulled out a brand new tricycle.

I noticed that Bartholomew had dislodged a photograph of a rather stern gentleman in a tweed suit and bowler hat. I asked Bartholomew who it was.

'I'm not altogether certain. Mummy seemed a little vague about it. Sometimes she suggested the man was Daddy. Other times she denied it. I draw the inductive inference that the photograph was given to Mummy by her own mother claiming that it was her absent father. As you suggested earlier, this is all part of some system to impose so-called moral restrictions. This photograph has probably been 'handed down' through countless generations. I should think it is ancient. I dread to think of all the people who have lived out their childhoods in misery, expecting this ugly brute to jump out of the bushes at the first hint of an illicit tinkle.'

Bartholomew contemptuously tossed the picture back into the bottom of the wardrobe.

He carried the tricycle into the nursery.

We peered into the kitchen cupboard. There was an impressive range of food for the party. Bottles of fizzy drinks, packets of liquorice torpedoes, jelly babies. Bartholomew snatched up handfuls of peanuts and sweets, and rammed them into his mouth. He opened one of the bottles and took a long swig.

'The effects will soon take place. I will then be able to demonstrate further fruits of my enquiries.'

We sat in the nursery and waited.

A small wind started to whine from Bartholomew's bottom.

Bartholomew nodded gravely.

'The time is right.'

He climbed onto his tricycle. The whine turned into a howl and the tricycle moved forward a few inches.

'See, the same principle of perfection that controls THE MISSILE and THE DETONATION controls the motion of the tricycle. As gases are ejected backwards, through my rectum, from the simple law that 'action and reaction are equal and opposite' it becomes a certainty that my whole body is going to be projected forward.'

But you've hardly moved.

Before I'd finished making my comment, the howl turned into a roar and the tricycle sped away.

Bartholomew made several loops around the nursery and then zoomed through the door. I heard him enter each of the bedrooms, the bathroom, followed by a heavy rattling as he descended the stairs. The sound diminished into the distance as he passed from the hall into the living room, from the living room into the dining room, from the dining room into the kitchen. The sound started to increase again as he returned from the kitchen, through the hall and back up the stairs to the nursery.

He swerved to a halt beside me.

'See. A practised ability to control the sphincter muscles of the rectum allows me a full control of the vehicle.'

Bartholomew's face was red and he was breathing deeply. I felt quite worried about him. The pupils of his eyes were dilated from the exhilaration of the velocity. His voice was babbling, more than usual, from the effect of adrenaline pumping into his blood stream.

'Don't you see. Don't you see. There's meaning to all this. There's a hidden plan. It's all going somewhere. It's all leading to a terrific end. Leading toward the ULTIMATE EXPERIENCE.

'Why does the anus happen to be placed at the rear of the body rather than the front? Have you not considered this subtle point? Isn't it obvious? THE TRICYCLE WOULD HAVE GONE BACKWARD OTHERWISE. It was intended that it should go forward all along. Why are my ears level with the bridge of my nose? On the off-chance that I might have to wear spectacles. I can extrapolate this principle into uncharted terrain. Answer me this, why am I in the possession of a MISSILE if Constantine cannot accommodate it?

'I have heard it said that miracles are violations of the laws of nature. I have heard it said that the evidence supporting the existence of miracles is at best fleeting. Well, I put to you the converse, that miracles actually form the underlying principle of nature. How come, when I faced the wilderness following my third birthday, when I first realised the harrowing emptiness of existence, I discovered the pleasures of the MISSILE? How come, when I found the tricycle in the wardrobe pending my fourth birthday and in horror anticipated the hours of pedalling the bloody thing, how come I discovered the locomotive gases? This is no coincidence. This is the proof of miracles. The proof that the laws of nature are miraculously ordered to satisfy our pleasures and needs. The purpose of our existence on this planet is to exploit the miracles for whatever we can squeeze out of them.

'Tomorrow, the day of my birthday, it is going to be the day of the ULTIMATE EXPERIENCE.

'It will be Saturday and Constantine will be waiting for Scarratt. But there isn't a Scarratt anymore. Instead, I will arrive on my powered tricycle and achieve union with Constantine. Afterwards I will invite Constantine and Wilberforce back here for the birthday tea party in order to celebrate.'

The anus began to roar.

The MISSILE rose on its invisible launcher.

As Bartholomew began to screw all the toys in the nursery, I feared he might inadvertently open up an evolutionary corridor and admit a disease that not even a dose of cod liver oil would put right.

Exhausted from his revelry, Bartholomew lay among the wreckage of the nursery. In the early hours of the morning something started to bump around the inside of the light-shade. Bartholomew opened his eyes.

'A moth.'

He jumped to his feet.

'I hate moths. Especially the big black ones that crash around the room.'

Apart from the one in the light-shade, there were two other moths, one crawling on the ceiling and the other stationary.

The stationary moth unexpectedly took to flight, causing Bartholomew to duck with his hands covering his ears.

'I'm leaving the room.'

He opened the door to the landing. The walls and ceiling were black with moths. The light was dingy and orange due to the presence of the insects crawling on the light bulb.

He started to whack them with a rolled-up comic. As they fell dead in thousands, more appeared. As he thrashed away, Bartholomew's face bore an expression of horror and disbelief.

'I've no idea where they're coming from.'

I suggested that maybe there was a window open somewhere.

'Oh, yes. Mummy tended to leave the windows open because of my empirical investigations. I suppose the lights being on during my revelry has attracted them.'

Bartholomew went round shutting the windows.

When all the moths were dead, he gingerly stepped over the piles of corpses.

I remarked that not all of the consequences of his actions led to results that supported his belief of final perfection.

Bartholomew looked a little sullen.

He looked through the window of the nursery with its view of the garden. The area where Wilberforce had dug the pit for Scarratt was hidden in darkness. Like puffs of steam escaping from a demented teapot I could hear grunts being emitted at regular intervals.

'Barth.'

'Barth.'

'Barth.'

'Barth.'

The scene was bleak and forbidding. It seemed an ideal moment to point out to Bartholomew the shortcomings of his scheme.

I reminded Bartholomew of his disappointment when he spliced Mummy in two. He had complained that owing to the presence of unforeseen organs, the symmetry was spoiled. I suggested that this might serve as a counter example to his principle of underlying perfection.

Bartholomew looked uncertain.

'Maybe we'd better check again, I could have been mistaken. It's probably just a matter of making a small adjustment.'

We went downstairs to the kitchen.

Something had changed. One half of Mummy was missing.

Fully clothed, Bartholomew lay in the cold, unmade cot.

'No, I cannot explain Mummy's partial disappearance. Mummy's partial disappearance means I cannot reassess the quality of symmetry of the 'final cut.' I really could do without these problems revolving endlessly in my mind. Tomorrow is my big day and I need to get to sleep.

After a lot of tossing and turning Bartholomew, his thumb in his mouth, started to drift to sleep.

Suddenly his eyes opened.

'Suppose the missing half of Mummy wasn't properly dead and, while I was revelling, slithered out to inform the man in the photograph, from the wardrobe, of my activities.

Bartholomew sucked harder on his thumb.

For the rest of the night, as the various possibilities raged in Bartholomew's mind, his eyes darted between the clusters of shadows that had gathered in the nursery.

The Grand Finale

Bartholomew sat at the breakfast table devouring a large bowl of Rice Krispies. Wilberforce watched from the opposite side of the table, his hand pressed into his cheek, forcing a fold of skin to almost cover his eye. Bartholomew was actually sitting on Wilberforce's book of wild flowers.

Bartholomew threw his spoon into the empty bowl.

'Now is the decisive moment.'

He tanked up on fuel and climbed onto his tricycle.

'O.K. O.K. It's time for the fireworks with Constantine. If my 'Mickey Mouse' watch is correct, she'll be waiting for Scarratt. When I arrive instead, think how impressed she'll be with my mode of powered transport. She will be irresistibly drawn to THE MISSILE. She will experience the HUNGER and then the SATISFACTION. We will unite and she will be mine forever. Then we'll come back here, light up the birthday cake and have a party."

Bartholomew sped up the path in the sunshine of his birthday.

Wilberforce edged his hand toward the forgotten book of pressed wild flowers. His fingers touched the red leather binding. Seemingly the book opened of its own accord.

Great Burnett. Sorrel. Fools Parsley.

He carefully sniffed the ends of his fingers as if they'd picked up the fragrance of cut meadows, still present in the parchment of the flowers.

His eyes darted from the book to the open door.

Quickly he snatched up the book and ran for the door.

It was too late. Bartholomew was already driving back up the garden path. Wilberforce returned the book to the chair and sat down again at the table.

Bartholomew stormed through the door and slammed it shut angrily. He had a large bruise just beginning to swell under his left eye.

'Purple buggery. It's all gone wrong. Yes, I discovered Constantine had a reciprocal feature to my MISSILE but would you believe it, it was the wrong bloody size. In fact, rather unreasonably, she took exception to THE MISSILE and walloped me in the eye. Worse than that, the little cow ran off to tell her mother. I think we can expect a visit from Mrs Pugh.'

Bartholomew ran to the refrigerator and removed the cake.

He erected the four candles.

'We've got to bring the party forward, then I've got to make my getaway. What with the thing with Constantine and half of Mummy on the kitchen floor I'm not sure I can explain everything. I'm not to be beaten though. I shall speed off towards the horizon leaving Mrs Pugh miles behind on her ancient push-bike.'

He consumed fuel for his journey and then lit the candles, sadly watching the red wax trickle down the sides.

'I really believed everything was going to work out in the end. I thought it was going to be THE GRAND FINALE.'

The flames of the candles started to jump and make popping sounds.

'Wait. Something's happening. Maybe this is going to be it. The final piece of the jig-saw puzzle. The event that will put everything in context and solve all my problems.'

Bartholomew watched the candles with fascination.

The flames began to give birth to smaller blue flames. The blue flames joined together into one globe of blue fire. The globe of blue fire wobbled in the air above the cake for a few seconds and then suddenly expanded to fill the dimensions of the room. Everything blackened. Bartholomew and Wilberforce's hair singed. The chairs, curtains and carpet charred. Wilberforce's book of wild flowers disintegrated into a pile of ashes.

The globe of blue fire gradually shrank, orbiting the room in erratic spirals like a deflating balloon. Finally, it shot up Bartholomew's anus.

He jumped to his feet slapping his backside.

'Ouch. Ouch.'

Wilberforce looked in horror at the remnants of his book of pressed wild flowers. Huge sobs began to well up and he ran out of the door.

Bartholomew sank onto the floor.

'What happened?'

All the windows were closed and I think there was a build-up of locomotive gases.

'Oh Christ, we're going to get a visit from Wilberforce's mother as well as Mrs Pugh.'

I looked out of the window. A more interesting throng was gathering than Bartholomew had envisaged.

Indeed, there was Mrs Pugh and Wilberforce's mother talking to each other at the garden gate. Also joining them was a policeman escorting Mrs Scarratt. Mrs Scarratt was holding the rather soiled infant Scarratt by the hand.

More intriguingly, a stern gentleman in a bowler hat arrived. I believe this was the man in the photograph we'd found in the wardrobe.

Bartholomew groaned with more than physical pain.

He turned to me.

'I still have you. Whatever happens I still have one friend.'

But Bartholomew I'm just your imaginary friend. I don't even exist. All my doubts, comments, criticisms and queries were yours, but you took little notice. You're quite, quite alone.'

My last impression of Bartholomew was of him wearing his new khaki shorts for the summer. Now they were torn, burnt, covered with soot, stained with oil from his tricycle and smeared with semen.

As the angry crowd converged on Bartholomew he began to cry.

Brethren of the Snout

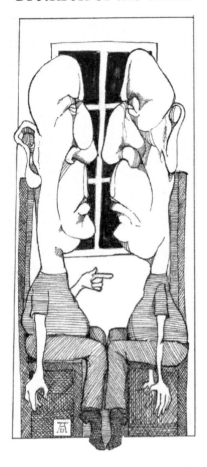

For some time, McNulty has been bullying me.

And his means? Simply sniffing. That is, a particularly loud, intimidating sniffing which has caused me much stress and more than a degree of physical pain.

Now McNulty has a bad cold and I believe his intent has turned to murder.

I must explain something of our situation.

McNulty is my lodger. I own a two-bedroom terrace house in a run-down area in the north of the country. I'm not able to work for reasons that I am unable to divulge, even to myself, and thus I'm not eligible for social security. Nor apparently am I sick. I thus require some form of income to remain alive. I sincerely thought that McNulty could provide this income. I believed he was in employment but came to suspect that his contribution to the GDP was relatively small.

The trouble is that I forgot to ask.

McNulty turned up on my doorstep one damp, chilly Saturday in November. It was not by chance. He was answering an ad that I'd put in the local post office for a lodger.

I felt that I had to interview McNulty to see if he was suitable. It failed to occur to me to ask for two references from respected members of the community. It wasn't the only thing that I forgot to ask.

We sat opposite each other.

McNulty sat with his legs wide apart. Naturally I presumed that this was to imply that he had big balls. I sat with my legs even wider apart to suggest I had even bigger balls. However, I came to doubt this inference when I noticed at a later point in time that his legs were clamped together tightly, as if the contents of his scrotal sac were so meagre that they required little or no practical consideration.

I looked down and noticed that I'd subconsciously adopted the same posture.

I asked McNulty to divulge all relevant information regarding his history that would help me discern if he was a suitable housemate.

Both his parents had just died and he had nowhere to live. Apparently, his mother was an award-winning baker and his father was bearded. His mother died in a shocking baking accident that was reported on the national news. McNulty provided the long details which caused me to have stomach cramps. His father shaved off his beard for the funeral and found that it revealed a malignant growth on the underside of his chin. The tumour immediately multiplied and sped to his extremities. He died an astonishingly brief four weeks later.

'Shame he shaved off the beard. If he hadn't, the tumour wouldn't have come to light and he needn't have died.'

I didn't feel I was on firm ground with this observation but McNulty nodded strong affirmation.

The result of this was that since his parents' house was rented, he couldn't afford to keep it on and he was now sleeping on the settee of an acquaintance from his schooldays.

Maybe I should have asked him if he worked and if he had sufficient income to pay the rent but instead, he began to question me. I supposed that that was fair enough. Living with someone is a two-way thing.

'Is this your house?'

'No it belonged to my mother.'

'And she died in a work-related accident?'

'No, she left me.'

'She left you?'

'For another son.'

That seemed to satisfy McNulty.

I didn't want to go as far as saying that I couldn't pay for the place without a tenant so I kept away from financial matters, to my detriment as it turned out.

Anyway, that seemed to wrap it all up and I offered him the tenancy.

I really had no idea of the future difficulties that that was to cause.

The only small clue was the brief appearance of a semi-luminous globe in one of McNulty's nostrils before he quickly snuffed it back up by a short, efficient input of air. I hardly noticed the sympathetic movement of air in my own nasal passage.

McNulty passed an absent-minded finger across his nose to check that it was suitably dry.

McNulty moved in the next day with the unasked questions still unanswered.

I worked on it over the next two weeks. McNulty inadvertently revealed two interesting facts that appear relevant to the nature of his occupation:

The first was that McNulty has calluses on his knees.

I learned this when I was forced to spy on McNulty whilst he was in a state of nakedness. I should make it clear that my spying on McNulty in a state of nakedness has no sinister implication whatsoever. I was forced to assess the full state of his physical situation in order to fill in the gaps resulting from the deficiencies of my interviewing technique. Was there a relevant physical abnormality to throw light on the matter? It turned out there wasn't. He was physically unremarkable apart from being a bit gaunt. But the calluses on his knees suggested he was accustomed to kneeling a lot.

The second fact was that McNulty has an irrational hatred of homeless people.

I discovered this when he resorted to Irn-Bru which appeared to be his main source of sustenance as far as I could tell, and a kind of latent hatred of the deprived came to the forefront. This appeared to be the only thing he was passionate about.

I simply put the two facts together and filled the gaping holes with wild speculations. I assumed the calluses on the knees were due to his kneeling on hard floors. I came to the conclusion that he cleaned the toilets and general facilities of a well-known charitable institution that provides support for homeless people.

I should point out that McNulty and myself are hardly thriving specimens of humanity. We are both young but bear the stigmata and shuffling postures of old men. In a kinder society we would be provided with free health care and meals on wheels.

We really needed cheerful servile women, to support us and become our wives.

Some chance of that.

It turned out that McNulty had diverted to a more ruthless mode of existence.

The first thing that I noticed about McNulty that worried me was the state of the kitchen cupboard.

It was empty.

As I've already mentioned McNulty seemed to be living on almost nothing.

When I pointed out the emptiness of the cupboard he explained in his droning, nasally voice how and why he managed on so little. I hid the fact that I was worried about the sufficiency of his income. It turned out that he, by astonishing physical application over time, had developed a rumen. I was impressed. At this point I really began to warm to McNulty.

'What's a rumen?'

I really had no idea.

'It's an extra stomach possessed by ruminants that gives them the capacity to digest grass, shoots and leaves and things that a human stomach would be unable to process.'

'What's a ruminant?'

'Like sheep and cows.'

'Horses and pigs?'

'No, just sheep and cows.'

'Not goats?'

'No.'

'Kangaroos?'

'No, just sheep and cows.'

McNulty certainly knows his ruminants.

Apparently, he started by eating strips of white paper from a shredder at his place of work (he did not elaborate further on this matter). His stimulus was nothing more than curiosity. Could he develop the capacity to fully digest paper? The paper naturally caused him to retch. The half-masticated paper was regurgitated back into his mouth. He chewed it some more and managed to swallow it again. Up it came for a second time. This went on for several regurgitations. The paper ended up an indigestible sludge. McNulty realised that he required more than the natural juices of the stomach to digest it. This was the moment of pure genius. He realised that by swallowing bacteria from a source he was unwilling to divulge, along with the pulp, he found that over time it started to break down to a state that his natural stomach juices could cope with.

'So, what do you eat now?'

'Mainly wood. As long as it's in small enough pieces I can usually digest it.'

This certainly explained how he managed to survive on such an empty cupboard. Naturally, I had a few reservations about McNulty's account but, like all good men, I believe whatever I'm told and don't argue against it. But privately I had one or two niggling questions:

If his mode of digestion was so successful, why was he so wasted and frail?

And for a person to have the ingenuity to develop a rumen would surely require some degree of genius. Was McNulty capable of genius?

This was our first proper conversation.

I became more aware of McNulty's sniffing and the effect it was having on my own respiratory system:

His persistent sniffing caused me to do likewise and my nasal passages were becoming sore.

I tried to take no notice.

Perhaps I too would be able to develop a rumen and live on next to nothing. Certainly, I had to do something fairly drastic to solve my predicament.

Two weeks into his tenancy it was undeniable that McNulty's sniffing was affecting my own breathing. I found my eyelid starting to twitch as if we were now connected by an invisible thread. I ignored it. McNulty appeared to be oblivious to the effect his sniffing was having on me. Everything on the surface remained cordial.

It turned out that McNulty had travelled in the Far East. I was unable to match this. The only thing I could say about travel was that I knew a bloke who had smuggled drugs across Morocco. To keep up with McNulty I made the most out of this story but in honesty I hardly knew the bloke. I got to know him vaguely when I sold him a television (again through an ad in the same post office that had alerted McNulty to the possibility of a tenancy in my house).

But it did make me suspicious of McNulty. Was his rumen a personal discovery? Had he in fact learned his unique method of digesting wood from yogis in the Orient? (or wherever he'd been).

Three weeks in and I noticed that the skin around my nostrils was becoming red and slightly inflamed. I also started suffering persistent sinus pain. I recognised that this was entirely due to the effect that McNulty's sniffing was having on me. If I remained in McNulty's presence for long enough the sinus pain developed into a headache then migraine. No amount of pills could shift the migraine. I imagined it must have been making McNulty's nasal passages as sore as my own.

I did start to wonder if all this was deliberate.

Four weeks into the tenancy our conversations had dried up because I was in too much pain. I was definitely losing the battle to cope with McNulty's sniffing.

I came to doubt that McNulty's breathing aberration was due to some congenital constriction of his nasal passages.

I was now certain it was all a deliberate ploy to destroy me. Whether it was his own invention or learned from yogis, it didn't matter. He had the means to kill me.

There would be one final gargantuan sniff and my head would split neatly into two equal parts. No doubt in the guise of a ruminant he would eat the sad remains and leave absolutely no trace. He would then assume my identity and take over my house.

As I watched McNulty manufacture stingy, irregular rollys in the kitchen, his sniffing became increasingly aggressive.

Sniff.

Sniff.

And sometimes it was more elongated.

Sniffffff.

But it didn't stop, except when pausing to make an even longer one. False hope would dawn and then:

Sniffffffffffffff.

When he smoked his rolly it was:

Puff/Sniff/Puff/Sniff/Puff with McNulty watching me all the time quite intently. Neither of us speaking.

Then I noticed a curious fact about McNulty. His eyes were watery. As I suspected, his own nasal passages must have been quite sore. He was clearly in an enormous amount of discomfort. This was going to turn into a battle of wits. Who could endure the most pain?

I should have asked McNulty simply to leave but by now I was too frightened.

The best thing was to avoid him. But he wised up to that.

I hid in my bedroom. But the sniffing just got louder. Even with my head beneath the pillow it penetrated my skull with deadly precision.

During the sixth week of McNulty's tenancy, when I believed that McNulty was out, I went in the kitchen to grab some food. My haste made me clumsy and slow but I had to get it done before McNulty returned.

As I was poised above the bread board with the bread knife in my hand, McNulty walked in.

'There's something I should say.'

There was an awkward pause and all that came out was:

Sniff.

Sniff.

Snifff.

Sniffff.

Sniffffff.

His eyes started to water and I could feel relentless stabbing in my nasal passages

I ran up the hall. McNulty followed me to the front door.

As I fumbled to open it, he spoke with astonishing innocence.

'I've caught a cold.'

This filled me with panic.

He might as well have said,

'It is time. You will now die.'

I'd expected my head to split but I was wrong. I felt a huge lump of mucus gathering in my trachea. I suddenly realised what McNulty was about to do. He was attempting to shift the mucus in my respiratory system to a convenient bottleneck in order to suffocate me.

I wrenched the front door open and sprinted up the street. I only paused to cough up the mucus onto the kerb and then I ran on.

I ran until the houses were no longer familiar. I ran through parks and along canals that I'd never encountered before. On and on. I resolved simply never to go back. It would be better to lose my house to McNulty than my life.

After an hour, exhausted, I sat down on a dustbin in an alley behind a row of terraced houses.

Suddenly it occurred to me that if I was homeless, I'd end up in the charitable institution that McNulty worked for. Leering, he would end my life with one short sharp sniff. I would have to move much further away. I stood up and looked at the dustbin. It looked very familiar. It had the same number, in fading white paint, as my own.

I had thought the wisest thing was to run so far that I simply got lost but inadvertently I must have gone in a circle and returned home.

I looked up. McNulty was standing over me looking red about the eyes and nose. I closed my eyes and prepared for the fatal sniff.

To my surprise I'd got nearly everything wrong.

And, to my surprise, I didn't die. Instead, I heard sobbing.

When I opened my eyes McNulty was crying. It turned out that his cupboard was bare because he was unemployed and not because he'd developed a rumen and was living off wood shavings. Apparently, he had been a cleaner at a charitable institution that helped homeless people but he'd been sacked for being rude to the clientele. He'd never developed a rumen or travelled in the Far East. He was very sorry that he'd lied to me and had not been able to pay any rent (I must admit I was so preoccupied with other things that I hadn't noticed this).

He thought that the problem between us was his not paying the rent and that I had rejected him. This was why his eyes were watery. He'd been very upset. It was the first time he'd actually had a proper friend. He was very sorry that his sniffing had caused me so much pain but he didn't realise that he did it. The upset he'd experienced when he thought I had rejected him had probably contributed to the sniffing but he was aware that, from childhood, he'd suffered from chronic catarrh.

This cleared the air and we found we could make a fresh start. I was glad because I'd felt that McNulty had been my first proper friend before it all went wrong.

McNulty suggested that we could address the problem by sniffing in exact unison. When he sniffed, I should sniff at exactly the same time and that might mask the effect. What was happening at the moment was that the sniffing induced in me was out of phase with his sniffing. It was the juddering reverberation that was causing the pain.

It took a lot of practise but McNulty turned out to be right. It was probably more difficult than learning to a play a musical instrument. We found that if we were at all out of step, by even a tiny increment of time, the pain returned, frequently accompanied by multiple nosebleeds.

Over months of hard work with hours of daily practice we achieved perfect unison and the project was astonishingly successful.

All pain had gone and I was largely unaware of McNulty's sniffing.

The only problem left was that neither of us had any income. But then McNulty made another discovery. There was a third bedroom. All the years that I'd lived in the house I never noticed the third door on the landing. This changed everything. We went to the post office and advertised for a second tenant.

A long line of hopefuls turned up. We were most pleased with young Petersen. He was a student at the local college and came from Worcester. Clearly his parents were loaded. As he filled the kitchen cupboard with a splendid feast McNulty sniffed slightly, as did I (now in perfect unison).

I could clearly see a momentary frown of pain imprint on Petersen's brow and he turned his head slightly to one side. A little patch of white appeared above the bridge of his nose, where the blood had drained away, before his naturally healthy complexion returned.

This was only the beginning.

We would be ruthless and unstoppable.

I could now see a prosperous future in which we walked down the street in sharp black suits and dark glasses. Yes, our tight drainpipe trousers would reveal little volume reserved for our balls but people would fear us nonetheless.

We were now the Brethren of the Snout.

Dialogue with a Pear

I've been staring at the pear in the corner for half an hour and still it hasn't said a word.

'I was always of the opinion that the inner workings of pears are too simple to sustain any form of sensible dialogue.'

It just needed something to break the ice.

'And we were always of the opinion that the inner workings of the human being are too complicated and messy to sustain any form of sensible dialogue.'

He/she/it, whatever, has a good point here. There certainly seems a lot of noise going on in there. But then I have been quite busy recently.

Let me summarise:

The acrobat from Amersham in the arboretum by arsenic.

The beautician from Barnsley in the bath with a Beretta.

The carol singer from Chichester in the cathedral by crossbow.

The dare-devil parachutist from Doncaster in the dumpster by dagger.

The evangelist from Everton in the elevator by extreme exfoliation.

And for those of you who haven't been reading the papers - I've done them all.

'And so you haven't got anybody to talk to because nobody likes you anymore. If they ever did. So, you had to turn to a pear as a last resort. Is it a case of the guilty mind needing to confess?'

I'm not going to let a pear intimidate me. Although he, it, she? --- what he says makes sense. Something might present itself as an 'it', but once you start a conversation with it, it seems awkward not to think of it in terms of gender.

'Look, are you male, female or what?'

'Does it matter?'

I suppose not really. This pear is making far too many pertinent points. I'm going to have to up my game or this pear will walk all over me.

The shadows are starting to deepen.

It's that sort of mellow moment in the late afternoon, in the winter, when old married couples consider drawing the curtains, building up the fire and having a cup of tea with a hobnob or a shortbread.

'And your thoughts turn to garrotting them.'

'That's completely unfair. How do you claim to know anything about me given that you appear to lack any organs of sense? I certainly can't see any peepers or lugholes.'

'Since you've been sitting there, my juices have turned quite sour. There's something definitely a bit off about you.'

'You mean you can taste your own juices?'

'I prefer the word 'sample'.'

'And you claim that such an internal process of recognition can provide a sufficient complex of meanings to allow you to discern my entire nature?'

'Seems to work for me. Is the nature of your work local in character or does it stretch to an international market?'

I discern no limitation:

The fire-eater from France in the furnace with a flame-gun.

The glue sniffer from Germany in the garden by gunpowder.

The halitosis sufferer from Holland in the hotel by (fatal) hysterics.

The igloo dweller from Iceland in the infirmary by ice-pick.

The juggler from Jamaica in the judiciary by (severed) jugular.

'You don't think that there's a pattern to all this that the police might latch on to?'

'As far as I'm aware, no. But then we tend to live in habits more than we like to admit. It usually takes others to spot them. None of us are as free as we like to imagine.'

'So, where do you think it might all end?'

'Why should it end?'

'I can see it ending with a resounding 'Z' and the police turning up to arrest you.'

'You discern an alphabet?'

'Not half. Something's got to give.'

'That's the test of genius, isn't it? Only a genius can make the pertinent shift to a new level to avert catastrophe.'

'And you think you've got what it takes.'

'I would like to think so. How's the juices going?'

'Sourer and sourer.'

Let me see if I can assist further:

The King of Kenya in the kitchen by killer bees.

The ladies-maid from Lyon in the lighthouse by lateral inversion.

The mathematician from the Manifold in the malt factory by malformation.

The nurse from Nuneaton in the neighbourhood by nitric acid.

The oligarch from Oslo in the outhouse by ossification.

The pear's now begging for me to stop.

'If you insist on telling me all this, then you're going to have to do me as well. When the police catch you, which they will, you can't expect me to keep quiet. I will tell them everything.'

'But there's no challenge in that. It's hardly the Pertinent Shift to do in a passive fruit. Where's the fun in that?'

'Which was the biggest challenge then? Which one is your favourite?'

The policeman from the Precinct in the patrol car by pratfall.

'You mean you've actually done one of their own kind? They're going to be salivating to get you. Members of the public are one thing but it's a completely different matter to do one of their own species.'

'That's right. I believe they've put the legendary Inspector Finch on the case. He's a ruthless solitary, much as myself, propelled instinctively by the pleasure of the moment. He chooses to work alone, not even trusting his fellow police officers. He's never been known to fail.'

The pear remained silent as if a vital flaw in my plan had been inadvertently uncovered. I changed the subject.

I tried to patch things up a bit.

'Each of my crimes has been committed without flaw. At the scene of each murder there was no evidence to link it to me. I'm not even a suspect. Nobody knows what I look like. Even Inspector Finch is in the dark.'

The pear still remains silent.

'So, when you go sour does it just affect you, or does it spread through the whole of your kind? Are all the pears in the world soured?'

'In this extreme case, it's not only souring there's also quite a bit of poison accumulating as well. Certainly, the longer I spend with you, the more toxic I become.'

'OK, does that mean that all the pears in the world become equally toxic.'

'Well, no. If that was the case, pears would have been regarded long ago as a poisonous fruit. The toxicity must only affect the fruit in the locality, probably not just pears. However, it maybe only affects fruit that have acquired language. I suspect that is quite rare. Maybe it is the element of discourse that introduces the poison.'

So, how's this for size?:

The quizmaster from Qatar in the quadrangle by quinsy.

The rat catcher from Rye in the round room by rupture.

The sunbather from Salisbury in the swimming pool by scorching.

The typist from Totnes in the twilight by tedium.

The upstart from urbanity in the u-bend by undernourishment.

'How's it going?'

'I've never felt worse.'

'On the outside you look fine. Delicious even.'

'I feel absolutely wretched. Where is this going? What are you planning?'

'I don't know what you mean.'

'Are you thinking of topping yourself? When Inspector Finch bursts through the door, you take one fatal bite and evade your captor forever.'

'Again, that would hardly be the Pertinent Shift. Just to take poison at the end. But it leads me to an intriguing thought. Surely the ultimate aim of the serial killer is simply be the last man (or woman, I'm not sexist). To exhaust the human race, once and for all, and go in ruthless pursuit of oneself. Think of the battle of wits that must ensue. Who could anticipate what would happen? The ending would be spellbinding, whatever the result. The hunter and hunted, as one, in a frenzied bid for survival.'

'Doesn't the paradoxical nature of your quest simply reveal that you are seriously imbalanced?'

'So, what are you aiming for? What is your telos? Just to ripen and submit to being eaten?'

'That's no longer a possibility whatever your view on the life-plans of pears. I am far too toxic now to achieve any such dream.'

But isn't there still room in there for more poison:

The vivisectionist from the veldt in the valley by vapour.

The werewolf from the Wirral in the wake by wager.

The xylophonist from Xanthus in the xystus by Xerox.

The yuppie from the YMCA in the yonder by Yahoo.

And finally:

The Zealot from Zanzibar at the zenith by zoetrope.

'Wait. There's something more to the last one isn't there?'

'What do you mean?'

'The Zealot wasn't dead, was he? You accidentally left him alive, didn't you? You didn't properly finish the job.'

'He was mortally wounded. He died later at the crime scene just as the police arrived. I realised that later. But he told them nothing, there wasn't time. How do you know this?'

'I'm just speculating. What is a 'zoetrope'?'

'It is a cylinder containing a sequence of images of a figure in motion. When the cylinder rotates you look through a slit and see the figure actually appearing to run.'

'And who was the figure in zealot's zoetrope?'

'I don't know.'

'Was it you?'

'Possibly.'

'And where were you running to in the zoetrope?'

'I have no idea.'

'Might it have been here?'

'Maybe.'

'To this address. Your home.'

'Maybe.'

'So, Inspector Finch now knows who you are? Where you were heading?'

'I suppose he might. But it is pure hypothesis.'

'Yet you knew the Zealot, he was your friend.'

'He was an acquaintance.'

'And he knew who you were and where you lived? By mistake you left him alive and he incorporated your image and address in his final zoetrope.'

'It's possible I suppose.'

'You calculated all of this. You indulged in a dialogue with me in order to make me poisonous. You are gambling that when Inspector Finch comes into the room, he will go straight to me and take out a bite. He will then drop dead and you will escape.'

'All policemen are pleasure-seekers. He has no choice.'

'Well, I think you are wrong. I think Inspector Finch is in strict pursuit and he will ignore me. Given the situation, he will be armed and I bet he will shoot you dead on sight. Think what he will see. A serial killer in earnest conversation with a pear? What will he think? Surely it reveals the full extent of your insanity. None of this conversation could have possibly happened. If you hadn't been talking to a pear for the last twenty minutes you could have escaped, with a head start, an hour ago. You've made a grave mistake.'

The door handle turns very quietly and Inspector Finch steps into the room.

The room is now only lit by the street light outside but it's enough to identify me.

He looks at me. There's definitely recognition.

As the pear suggested he would, he removes a handgun from his pocket.

But, as I anticipated, before pulling the trigger, he seizes the pear impulsively and takes a quick, sly bite out of it. A juice-releasing, saliva fuelled crunch. Hardly has he bitten in, he falls to the floor writhing, the gun unfired. The half-demolished pear rolls across the carpet, fluids dribbling from the disrupted flesh. I think it's in pain.

I have to have the last word of course.

I stand over the pear gloating.

'See I was right. Policemen are pleasure-seekers. But please appreciate the Pertinent Shift. This was to form a poison-inducing dialogue with a pear in the first place. Nobody has done that before. It is radical creation at its most potent. Whatever he made of the dialogue, whether he thought it to be real or just in my imagination, he couldn't have anticipated how toxic it had made you.'

I am sure that the pear would have responded by saying that, given the sickness of my mental state, I'd injected strychnine, or whatever, into the pear beforehand. But I don't have to put up with that banter anymore. The pear, along with Inspector Finch, has perished.

But note that I didn't murder the pear.

Ironically, Inspector Finch performed that feat.

I slip out of the door ready to conquer new alphabets and maybe eventually to achieve the final end of humankind.

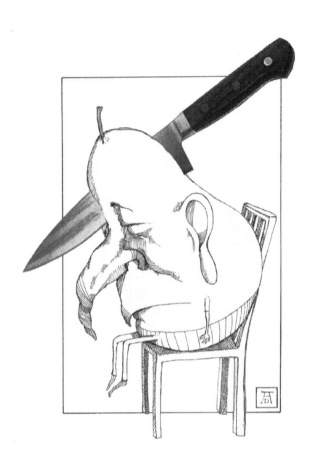

The Principle of Population

Since the late onslaught of the disease of neoliberalism, infection of the lungs has gone up a treat and childhood mortality has topped the previous records. Due to the latter, I presume, the size of families have bozoomed. I reckon that this is in order to preserve the population growth, to maintain economic prosperity (what with the greater multitude of twinkies croaking). Fair enough I suppose.

My own family is an excellent example of this.

I'm the middle child in a family of thirteen siblings. Here's the list (before I forget):

1. Baby Bumkins (still too young to have a determinate sex)

2. Infant Fretting (a bit of a pain in the rectilium if you ask my opinion)

3. Zulu (surprisingly a different colour but overall quite a nice chap)

4. Little Pippa (my favourite because she's so sweet)

5. Tiny Tom (small in stature but a big prick in irritational terms and wets the bed, something we all regret)

6. Bigger Pippa (obviously bigger than Little Pippa but lacking the sweetness)

7. Dick the Clever (that's me –the only one that can write)

8. Pauline the Hun (I think she's a feminist, she certainly doesn't like me or any of my brothers)

9. George the Large (one pudding too many and all that)

10. George the Larger (twenty puddings too many I suspect)

11. George the even Larger (apparently due not to puddings but a sluggish metabolism but I think there's more to it)

12. Pouting Pru (with enormous mammaries but we're not allowed to touch)

13. Roger (reliable sort of bloke but lacking furniture in some of the upstairs rooms but then he has had trouble with his hormones and has recently suffered a massive growth spurt)

It might be thought that the numbering that I have included in the above list is due to the meticulous care I have put into the ordering of this information. This is incorrect. The numbering relates simply to the age of each child. By pure coincidence, chronologically, we are each separated by exactly one year.

So, how did it happen that each of us was to succumb to infant mortality?

The fundamental cause was pyromania. It seems to run in my father's family. Certainly, his brother came home drunk late one night, put the chip pan on and promptly went to bed. The whole lot went up. Wife and thirteen kids done for. As so often happens, the perpetrator of the misdeed was the sole survivor.

My father's effort was however far more modest. Our mother summed it up well.

'Your father's burnt a hole in the carpet and I'm either too busy or too tired to mend it.'

I believe he was lighting his pipe from a burning coal from the fire by means of tongs. Again, he was under the influence of drink and maybe it wasn't the best moment to be practising such an ambitious manoeuvre. There were no witnesses but I presume the coal fell unnoticed onto the carpet and was left to smoulder while my father staggered off to bed (whether the pipe was smoked or simply abandoned, I have no idea).

Unlike his brother's case it didn't lead to a full house fire but just the carpet preferred to smoulder. The next morning there was a small black hole in the carpet by the hearth and the ammoniac stench of scorched fibres and charcoal.

When we poked the hole, we realised that it had gone all the way through the floorboards into the void beneath the house. I'd say it was about two inches across and implied no threat to the occupants.

As indicated it was largely ignored.

Life continued much the same with the hole as without it. Little Pippa said she thought it was getting bigger and this point was endorsed by Pauline. I think that was because she thought Father should have done more to correct it and also, she was highly critical of Father's nature in general and for causing the fire in the first place. Father and mother denied it but this became difficult when Baby Bumkin disappeared.

We looked all round the house and even shone a light down the hole.

It seemed a bit sinister.

Baby Bumkin was definitely in the room. And the hole by now was certainly bigger. Big enough to swallow Baby Bumkin.

Father pressed his face to the hole to the extent that for some time afterwards his eyes, nose and mouth were inscribed in a red circle. He peered for ages. All we could see was a massive, massive palpitating arse. I expected any moment for the floor to be ripped up and Baby Bumkin, dead or alive, to be extracted from the void beneath the house. I don't know what he saw but when Father stood up, he looked disturbed. I always meant to ask him what he'd actually seen.

He simply said,

'Baby Bumkin's gone for good.'

There was wailing and remorse. To emphasise that the search was over Father hastily nailed pieces of crudely sawn wood over the hole with bent and rusty nails.

His brother came over to give advice. Of course, he was an expert in this sort of situation.

'Don't inform the police. They will automatically assume that it was an inside job, the parents will be arrested and imprisoned for infanticide and the kiddies divided up among as many foster homes as the number of survivors' permit.'

It was agreed that it was best to maintain the principle of population and for our parents to simply go for another baby as soon possible and pass it off as Baby Bumkin.

A few weeks went by and gradually the laughter of children returned to the house.

Little Pippa was calling,

'Come quick, Infant Fretting is about to take her first steps.'

By the time we got there, Little Pippa was crouched on the floor, whimpering. The hole, slightly enlarged, had re-emerged. I had a sense of smouldering round the perimeter rather like with a forgotten cigarette in an ashtray. The boards that Father had nailed over it had seemingly disintegrated, there was just a burning smell in the room. I was aware that the smell of burning had never really totally gone away.

There was no sign of Infant Fretting.

Father nailed more and more wood over the hole in a frenzied motion. He padlocked the door and forbade anybody to enter.

Life was now much harder in our house of two bedrooms. We in our cramped dormitory trying to maintain the joy of childhood and Father and Mother in the next room attempting to secure the Principle of Population.

Presumably this was turning into an arduous task.

At least we all thought we were safe.

Then quite unexpectedly one night we had all just gone to bed when the lights went out. It was as if somebody had drawn breath and sucked in the electricity of the house. We remained for about a minute in absolute darkness everyone drawing breath unable even to murmur. The lights came on again but Zulu was no longer there. The brave little warrior had gone. Frantically we called for Father and Mother who searched every corner of the room.

We went downstairs. The door of the living room was open and the hole was enlarged and gaping like a hideous mouth issuing an acrid vapour.

This time, Father bricked up the doorway and nobody was ever able to enter the room again.

Among the siblings there was, to some extent, a feeling that our parents still weren't doing enough to protect us. Pauline was most critical of Father. But there was some agreement that nobody would want to come and live in this house so a swap was out of the question.

Quite quickly Little Pippa followed Zulu. This caused me genuine pain because as I've already mentioned, Little Pippa was my personal favourite. With her little dolly, red shoes and party frock with no party ever to go to. I wailed and wailed but she never came back.

The fact that the door was now bricked up made no difference whatsoever.

Then it was Tiny Tom. No great loss there but we certainly went through the motions of grief. Actually, it turned out more evocative than that. At the time, Tiny Tom was wearing his cowboy suit with floppy holsters containing cap guns and a tear in the trousers with his arse hanging out. When I thought of the cowboy suit, I did feel my eyes pricking. It had once been mine but ironically, I'd grown out of it.

It was at this point that it occurred to me that a pattern was emerging. Maybe nobody else had noticed it. But, if I was right, things looked bad for Bigger Pippa. Again, I don't think Bigger Pippa would have been a huge loss but then it meant that I would be next. Me. That was definitely not good. I needed a plan.

Maybe I'm mistaken but I think this whole thing is simply moving in the direction of size and the relative ease of falling down a widening hole. If I can make myself bigger, at least for the moment, bigger than Pauline then I have a safety margin. Although, looking ahead, the trio of ever-increasing Georges might present something of a challenge. I'll have to worry about that later.

But after all we live in a Darwinian universe. It is my duty to survive however ruthless it may seem.

But what would my means be?

Since five had disappeared that meant that there was more food about than there had been before. Humans are creatures of strict habits. I doubt if my mother had fully adjusted to the losses and was churning out the same quantities of food as before. She probably just binned the uneaten surplus without noticing.

Certainly, in the cupboard there was quite an accumulation of Baby Bumkins' pots of bland splop. In the middle of the night when everybody was out of the way I made a start. I consumed as much as I could before I started to wretch.

I was right that Mother was preparing the same quantity of food as before. I made sure I surreptitiously had seconds, thirds, fourths and fifths. This helped maintain my mother's habit of overproduction.

I was lucky (so much is down to luck) that the disappearance of Bigger Pippa didn't take place for a few weeks. By the time she did disappear I was quite a lot bigger than Pauline (although not still as big as George the Large). I was definitely not next in line.

Bigger Pippa as I expected went without fuss. On the pluses there was more food available. On the minuses it was quite a tense time for me. Maybe my theory was wrong and that some factor other than size governed the disappearances. I remembered, after Baby Bumkins vanished, my father's expression after he'd looked down the hole. I wondered again what he'd seen but somehow didn't manage to ask him.

The tension went on for longer than I hoped.

Suddenly Pauline was no longer there. I leapt for joy before landing in a crumpled distraught heap. I had survived. My plan was working. But Pauline's exit brought new rewards. Not only more food but a formerly unrevealed laptop with internet connections that she used to contact her lesbian-feminist friends in order to fuel her hatred of Father. This may come in useful in the future. I now had contact with the world beyond.

I had survived but the task ahead of me was formidable. The three Georges looked fairly unmoveable. I watched them carefully at the dining table, spooning in pudding. I used to think my parents giving three consecutive siblings the same name showed astonishing ineptitude and perhaps an astonishing lapse of memory. But now I always think of the three Georges as essentially the same person, but in different stages of fatness. I mean, other than the fatness, there is nothing to distinguish them. Same voice, same hair, same teeth, same mannerisms, same whatever. The only variance pertains to the measure of the abdomen.

I reckoned I was fairly even, at this moment, with George the Large but I suspected that I'd just slightly moved ahead. But if George the Larger had looked pretty stiff competition as for George the even Larger, I felt somewhat overwhelmed. I'd long run out of Baby Bumkins' splop and the extra nosh that Pauline released was disappointing to say the least.

It turned out that I was right about George the Large. He went next without any problem. I was astonished by how much extra food became available to me. But as George the Larger loomed ahead I knew for definite that I was the next man down the hole and I had to get chomping.

I chomped and chomped and chomped.

You can never be that sure that you've done enough to avoid the ultimate relegation. It was a tense few weeks but then I had the good idea to put him in for the interschool cross-country run. Despite protestations he wasn't allowed to pull out and the following morning after the run George the Larger was successfully dispatched. It was the merry, merry month of October. Well, it was a merry month for me at least.

I now had to face George the even Larger. As I intimated earlier, George the even Larger was a bit of an enigma. Unlike the other Georges, he ate relatively little. His vastness was apparently due to a sluggish metabolism.

He seemed to be quite matter of fact about it all.

'Well, Rupert, it's either me or you next.'

He couldn't even remember my name. It's Dick. Dick. Dick. Dick.

'But I'm confident that I'm the bigger of the two of us. And I'm confident that I will remain so.'

Though he was irritating me, he might be right.

This point of irritation spurred me on (he definitely had to go) but I needed something more than what was available to gazump George the even Larger's girth.

Then I made an amazing discovery. While I was performing a routine midnight exploration, I came across George the even Larger's secret.

Scrambling beneath the fairly extensive section of the bed George slept on, I found a number of secret compartments cut into the underside of the mattress.

They were full of sweets, crisps and chocolate.

I gathered the source of his largeness and put it in a safe place and started in earnest to change the balance of the situation.

The next morning, George the even Larger, knew what had happened. The way he looked at me I could tell he knew who had pinched his stash but he couldn't say anything. As I grew before his very eyes, he obviously felt some pressure to replace his stash as quickly as possible. However, it was too late. Before he succeeded in this, he was summoned by the hole and consumed.

This left me with the knotty problem of Pouting Pru.

It was clear cut that I was weightier than Pru (at least by a factor of two). But with Pru, it wasn't a question of the weight of the flesh but the distribution of flesh. It was the sheer volume of the jugs that was putting my life in jeopardy.

I had completely consumed George the even Larger's stash but I wasn't coming near to competing with Pru's extended circumferences and I started to sink into a despair that I'd never known before.

However, luck came from the most astonishing direction. My body rebelled against the abuse that I was subjecting myself to. I experience appalling stomach cramps and my abdomen swelled out alarmingly with sufficient gases to power a manned spacecraft to the moon. While I was rolling about in agony, Pauline departed and that left just Roger.

Simply Roger. Simple Roger. Roger the Simple. Roger of the recent growth spurt. Roger the lank.

Then the anomaly of Roger struck me. Roger the Anomalous. Although Roger had recently had a growth spurt he hardly had the hole stopping qualities of the three Georges let alone Pauline. He was the stereotypical beanstalk.

But where was Roger? Nobody had seen him for some time. Nobody noticed that he'd long gone. Long gone. Everybody (including myself) had become fixated so much on the order of things that we failed to notice that Roger had succumbed at a prior point in time. I suspect he departed sometime between Pauline the Hun and George the large.

Rather illogically I thought my task was done.

But surely the parents are still children. I thought of them in the next bedroom, banging away. Nobly attempting to maintain the Principle of Population whatever the cost to themselves.

But what progress had they made? So far they hadn't managed to replace even Baby Bumkins let alone any of the others.

Mother was pregnant and she had noticeably swelled out.

But I had overtaken her. It was no competition. If she was a candidate for the hole then she would be next.

And she was.

It just left Father and me.

The task was now relatively simple. Although father was the biggest of the big, in the loneliness, I joined him in his drinking. We drank stout mainly and lived off greasy chips from the chip shop. We passed many a drunken evening together smoking our pipes. It was all very pleasant.

I grew and grew.

We shared pretty much everything. We had identical diseases. Diabetes, high blood-pressure, arteriosclerosis, gout. We were not in good shape.

There was the question that I'd always meant to ask him after the disappearance of Baby Bumkins.

'So, Father. When Baby Bumkins first vanished down the hole and you looked down it for ages, you saw something that disturbed you but didn't say what it was that you saw. I always wondered about it. What was it?'

There was no reply. I looked round and saw that his chair was empty.

Just me now.

Expanding to survive.

How long can I keep this up? Dr Zum, a medical practitioner from the private sector who gives me pain killers and keeps me free of infection at some considerable cost, says I will soon come to a natural limit. This is the point where the inputs balance with the outputs and I will expand no more. Hence eventually the hole will catch up with me. I personally can't really see why there are any such limits. I think Dr Zum is being modest (or unnecessarily pessimistic). There will always be something he can give me to maintain a responsible level of growth in the unforeseeable future.

Cunningly, I have learned to maintain my expansion by forming lucrative internet businesses by means of Pauline's computer.

Although I am morbidly obese and cannot leave the house (or my bed even), food is brought directly by a paid lackey.

But it is all exhausting.

I look forward to a time in the near future maybe when I can take a wife and raise a family to release me, at least for a while, from the arduous task of perpetual expansion.

Odeur de Sainteté

On looking back it was a surprise to me that I was chosen to attend Tony Blair's autopsy, let alone perform it. I'm sure it is obvious that I wasn't the best qualified to carry out the task. As I sit in a small confined room, writing my account of the events, it seems a useful opportunity to reflect fully on what actually happened:

I was told, by letter, to attend a large room that looked like a derelict gymnasium at nine o'clock, Monday morning.

I reported to a woman sitting at the reception desk. It was all very cursory.

She asked me my name and ticked a register. She asked me if I carried a mobile phone or a watch.

All I had was a watch.

'It's the same one that I had as a child. A Timex. It doesn't have a second hand. It was a big disappointment to me back then. Well, it wasn't until I was saw Stephen Tuplin's watch. Both were Christmas presents. Stephen Tuplin's was luminous and had a second hand. It drew admiration from many quarters including my best friend's mother. Doesn't matter now of course. Stephen Tuplin's long gone on to better things and my best friend's mother is dead. As you see, the hands don't glow in the dark either. Still going though. Loses a minute or two every day but on the whole it works well. It's just a matter of remembering to move it on a bit every morning. I certainly wouldn't get another one unless it broke.'

I don't think she wanted to know any of this. She certainly showed no interest and simply asked me to hand it over. She attached a label to it with my name on it and placed it in a box with similar items belonging to other people and said that it would be returned at the end.

She asked me if I had a mobile phone or similar device, obviously with the intention of confiscating it.

'No. I'm hoping to get one for my birthday.'

Finally she asked me if I'd brought with me everything mentioned in the instructions of the letter. I hadn't fully read the letter and wasn't sure what she was referring to, so I nodded.

She told me to wait.

She was a fairly unpleasant-looking woman with one eye and she was wearing some sort of uniform. I thought it looked a bit like a nurse's uniform but then I'm no expert. In fact, I don't think it was.

I stood uncomfortably as people accumulated. It was only men and it was starting to be unruly. One bloke looked like a pantomime villain. With his henchman he set on a little roly-poly man with an impeccably groomed moustache and goatee. With gleeful laughter they tore off his clothes. The little bloke ended up naked and crying on the floor. He had the tiny penis of a cherub which contrasted strangely with the beard. Cherubs don't have goatees. It might have contrasted less if he'd had pubic hair. Oddly, I can't remember. That's one of the sort of things that people automatically notice but later deny any knowledge of the matter. In my case I can't deny looking but in all honesty I simply can't remember.

I felt the woman at the desk should have imposed some order but it was as if she had strategically positioned herself so that any occurrences in the room happened in the line of vision of her blind eye. She was busy with the register.

A little old lady, who I hadn't noticed before, stepped forward. She picked up the little man's clothes and led him off to a room at the back, he was still crying. She seemed very practised in her work and had a genuinely kindly manner. She wagged her forefinger at the pantomime villain but he ran off followed by his henchman, both issuing raucous laughter. He seemed to be enjoying himself enormously.

I began to feel nervous, worrying that they might set on me.

The proceedings began with the woman official standing up. At this point, the little man returned to the room fully clothed and looking much happier. The woman official started to call out names. The named individuals left the room.

Mine was fourth on the list. I felt relieved. Better to be away from all of this. Just as I was leaving I noticed that the pantomime villain had once again set on the little man. In an astonishingly small amount of time he stripped the clothes off him again.

He started to cry again.

My exit wasn't a moment too soon.

The named individuals gathered in a much smaller room. It was somebody's office in fact. It was Dr V's office. When people write accounts sometimes they leave out the surname I suppose for various reasons of discretion. In my case it is simply because I can't actually remember the name but I know he was some sort of doctor (I think).

Dr V was making light conversation as if answering a question that nobody had actually asked. It seemed very relaxed and friendly.

'Yes, of course some of the older ones of you might recall that this place was originally a workhouse. Its function has changed of course. In fact it's changed many times. It became a hospital for the sick, later it became a subnormality hospital. When the clientele was dispersed into the community it was given some other purpose and then after that something else. I must admit I'm a little vague on its later uses. When it was finally noticed how outmoded the place was, it was proposed that it should be knocked down. Most think it had gone years ago. But all this happened when heritage became all the rage. It was to be preserved for posterity, presumably to show how we mistreated the needier personages of society in the distant past. That explains the labyrinthine structure. The endless corridors etc. I hope none of you manage to get lost while you're here. I've worked here for two years and several times I've lost track of where I was. It can take a surprising amount of time to get your bearings again. My motto for this place is 'never be without your mobile."

Some of the other's automatically patted their pockets to check if their mobiles were there. But of course they'd all been handed in.

Dr V's sallow secretary gave each of us a clipboard with two trapped sheets of A5 paper and one of those cheap, scratchy biros that stop working long before the tube of ink has run out. By definition of being a twenty six year old I can't help taking note of the female presence (not that I'm noted for my success in this field, although I always have an unmoveable faith in The Procreative Scheme). Dr V's secretary looked as if she might have a secret disease lurking somewhere within. Leukaemia or Crohn's disease maybe. There's inevitably a downer at some strategic point or other in the desirability stakes. She also had a funny looking nose. It was a bit long and wonky. On the other hand, as she gave me the clipboard, our eyes briefly met and she smiled slightly I thought (I can't absolutely guarantee that happened –I might have imagined it, I usually do).

Dr V started to explain the nature of the task for which we had been selected.

I found some difficulty in concentrating because my attention was following the secretary as she continued to distribute the clipboards. I'm never good at concentrating whatever the circumstance. As Dr V's voice droned on, I noticed that she didn't smile at anybody else. No, there was definitely a lack of eye contact. This had to be significant.

But then the biro of one of the other clients failed to work and she was very pleasant and helpful in replacing it. There was a whispered exchange between them and she made an involuntary snort of laughter as she walked away. It makes a huge difference when someone laughs when you thought they were incapable of such a human trait. Not that I fancied her. But I recognised that she was more likely to fancy him. It was always like that for me. He did seem better looking than me. They did seem better suited. Or to put it more aptly, he looked less odd than I did.

I suddenly noticed that the light conversational tone had gone out of Dr V's voice and that he'd got onto more serious matters. In fact the voice was now quite cold and officious. That sort of quality that might almost be mistaken for barking in the distance.

Dr V appeared to be explaining that our appointment here was something to do with the recent terrorist atrocity that we'd no doubt heard about on the news.

I don't really follow the news. It always seems the case that there's just been a terrorist atrocity. Or there's just about to be one. People are always being killed in terrorist atrocities. It's easy to lose track of who's been killed by who. Maybe the other people in the room were better informed than me. They seemed to be nodding slightly. But on the other hand so was I.

Dr V's secretary returned to her seat. I'll have to call her Miss A. This time it was not due to lack of memory but simply because I never knew her name.

I looked around the room. I noticed that the henchman of the pantomime villain was sitting at the end of the row. He now seemed quite subdued. I noticed he had a slight twitch around the eyebrows and forehead. He seemed milder and less threatening now that he wasn't with his leader.

It started to strike me that everybody looked odd. It wasn't just me and the bloke whose pen didn't work. A little deficient as well. Some more than others. But we all seemed placed at the bleak end of the spectrum of plausibility.

Bits of what Dr V said come to light.

'This must not be seen as a voluntary task. It is a civic duty. Think of it as a variant of jury service but with more demands on you. If you refuse the task, even at this stage, prosecution is automatic. You will be arrested but you will not be sent for trial in an open court. The sentencing is harsh and automatic. Do you understand?'

Definitely.

I joined in the murmur of consent.

I looked across at Miss A. She seemed to be following closely what Dr V was saying. She bore a small frown of concentration. Surely she must already be familiar with his spiel, I suspected. I maintained my gaze, hoping for some reciprocation.

I must seem desperate. I am. Not that I fancy her (I must keep reiterating this fact). I desperately searched for some point of attraction in her. Her hair was light brown, thin and drawn back from her face. It was gathered in a little black band at the back of her head. I imagined that if it was released and shaken free it would be straggly and hardly reach the base of her neck. She wore a plain grey skirt that ended mid-calf. The little bit of bare leg that I could observe was mottled and shapeless. Her pallid face was completely without makeup. Not even a trace of lipstick. Nothing. Then I noticed she was wearing a thick bracelet. I think it was purple. So there was a single item of feminine decor on her wrist.

Dr V was still speaking somewhere in the background.

'Any information you might need is to be found in the Resource Centre. You have permission to use any of the books as long as you do not deface or make marks of reference in them. You are allowed to use the photocopying facilities in order to copy any section of a book that you might require, but a slip must be filled in and handed in immediately. These are available at the copier. There is a wide range of relevant online articles at your disposal. Again you may use the facilities to print any article that might be of use in completing your task. If you have difficulty accessing any information you must ask my secretary. She is your prime contact. She can be reached at all times by the device we will give you shortly. It cannot be used for speaking. It simply sends a signal. If she is not immediately available you will be put on hold. You must wait till she is ready to respond. Any documents that you print out or any notes you make must be handed in once the task is complete. Nothing whatsoever must be removed from the building. Needless to say that goes for samples of tissue or body parts. There will be no souvenirs. Do not begin to think about eBay. The reasons are obvious and do not require spelling out.'

That sounded a bit heavy but, on the other hand, Miss A's bracelet was definitely a revelation. Then I noticed her ears were pierced. There were tiny retainers, hardly visible, in the punctured lobes but no actual decorative earring. There was no ring on her fingers or anything like that. But then there might have been a trace of eye makeup after all. Originally I had thought definitely not. But now I'm beginning to think there is.

She was still listening hard to Dr V.

Why?

Then the penny dropped that it was Dr V that she fancied. He was predictably in a tired, loveless marriage. He was probably nobbing Miss A. But I knew he wasn't really devoted to her. Not as much as she was probably to him. These situations always turn out like that. Then it occurred to me that Dr V looked a bit odd as well. We were a conglomerate of oddities. Dr V was presumably permanently embittered because his career to date had failed to reflect his true value. But he was in denial that it was all because he was a bit odd. That was his real problem. It was a fact that was all too quickly picked up by colleagues and potential employers, I have no doubt. I bet he was picked out at school for being odd.

Dr V was still explaining things.

'You will operate between nine o clock and five o clock with a half hour break for lunch. You will return to your room when you are not involved with the task. During the task you must not speak to or contact anybody apart from myself or my secretary. You must not discuss any details even with my secretary, you can only discuss your immediate requirements pertaining to the task. All other conversation is strictly prohibited. All visits to the Resource Centre must be pre-agreed and adhere to a strict schedule to avoid contact with other people. If there is some breach of protocol due to whatever reason and you do meet somebody in a corridor, toilet, etc, do not make any contact. Do not speak. Report the incident immediately to my secretary. If you ignore this advice the retribution will be severe. Naturally you will not leave the building at any point during the task. This is the reason that you were asked to bring a bag containing overnight provisions and spare clothes.'

I looked round the room. Everybody else had some form of bag at their feet. I'd forgotten mine. This is what the unpleasant woman on the desk was referring to when she checked me in.

For me, this is a recurring theme. At the time it seems the easier option to be not completely honest. Saving face, maybe, when it really doesn't matter.

I didn't feel I could stand up at this stage and announce that I didn't have overnight things.

I did begin to wonder what all this was about.

'Before you go you will be given a security pass for the purpose of identification which you will attach to your lapel. This will not identify you but it will identify the status of the task you will perform. This will become clearer later. But for now you must realise that the tasks you are all facing are not of equal status and thus carry a different burden of responsibility. As you probably know, there were nineteen victims in all. There are four categories of priority. Category Four contains nine victims. Category Three contains five victims. Category Two contains four victims. Category One has just one. Let us say that Category One is the most politically sensitive category, the others are of less significance but remain important none the less. Obviously the tasks bearing higher status will receive more external monitoring. If there are cock ups or grounds for negligence, the retribution will be harshest for the higher categories. For this reason the status of the task you will perform is chosen on an entirely random basis. Our principal aim here is fairness. Once assigned there is no provision for appeal. I must reemphasise that if you fail in your task, for whatever reason, you will face punishment without trial, which will have serious implications for the rest of your lives. But I'm confident that that will not happen. If you would please stand in a line and collect your security pass. You will all make a start tomorrow at nine o clock. Good luck.'

We stood in a line. I was roughly half way along and Miss A handed out the passes from a dispenser on the desk.

I have always tended to have bad luck but for once I didn't. Miss A handed me my security pass. It was the Category One. Our eyes met again. This time the contact was definitely significant. Her eyes signalled urgency. Almost a sorrow. She was slightly shaking her head as if she might have doubted my reciprocation of her feelings.

I pinned the pass to my lapel.

I think I've pulled.

One by one we were taken to our rooms by Miss A. It took quite a bit of time.

I was the last. As we passed though seemingly endless corridors, disappointingly she didn't speak at all.

I completely lost all sense of direction. Miss A stopped at a door near the middle of one of the corridors and produced a key.

'I've forgotten to bring my bag.'

I sounded rather pathetic. My voice came out a bit scratchy and thin. It wasn't really the image that I wished to convey.

She seemed astonished and irritated.

'You mean you've left it in the meeting room?'

'No, I forgot it altogether.'

'Did you mention it to the receptionist?'

'No. I sort of gave the impression that I'd brought it.'

I definitely wasn't proving to be the sort of bloke that she would fancy.

'Why didn't you mention it earlier? They wouldn't have let you through. They would have probably dismissed you at the reception desk and they would have let you go home without any incrimination. But it's too late now. The tasks have been assigned so there's no going back. I don't know how they'll react. I'm breaking the rules but I'm off duty shortly and I'll bring back some of my brother's clothes.'

I went in the room. The door shut behind me and I heard the lock go.

'Suppose there's a fire?'

There was a pause. I wondered if she could still hear me.

'Then you'll burn. You're going to anyway.'

She was quite matter of fact about it all.

I listened to her footsteps returning up the corridor. I liked her sense of humour.

The room was small and bare. There was a small area to the right of the door with a sink and a tarnished mirror. There was a toilet with a disturbing stain streaking down the bowl right into the u-bend. It looked as if the toilet didn't really belong and had just been thrown in place as an afterthought. It wasn't behind a door or partition or anything. I flushed it to see if it was connected. An inadequate dribble of water went into the bowl and reluctantly drained away with a half-hearted swirl. It left the stain intact.

The cistern started to refill with a slow endless trickle.

The main part of the room was lit by a solitary white orb in the middle of the ceiling. There was a table with a chair and a rather small single bed with a hard mattress. And that was it. There was a crude wardrobe with a few dangling wire coat hangers. It divided the sink area from the rest of the room.

Next to the bed was a small scruffy mat made of that particularly coarse kind of material that never wears out. It was hardly a home comfort.

The table bore a microwave containing a nondescript ready-meal imbued with lethal levels of salt and saturated fats. Next to it was a jug of water with a trace of green algae round the base and rim. Also there was a green apple with a nasty bruise that was already showing traces of fungus and a blackened banana that belonged to the long dead.

A blind had been pulled down over the window. When I peeked beneath it I found the window was completely blocked off on the outside by breeze blocks. This is why the light was left on. There was no natural light whatsoever. I felt a bit claustrophobic in the locked, windowless room. The room felt hot and my mouth was dry. I struggled for a split second to recall the season. Was this an airless, hot summer's day? Or was it winter and the heating was jammed on the highest setting? There was no way to tell, apart from recourse to recent memory.

There was no glass so I had to drink straight from the jug. I think this was an oversight. The water was warm and I suspected it had been there for several days. I could have refilled it from the sink but I didn't know if it was drinking water and, in any case, the jug was too large to fit under the tap.

I placed my clipboard on the table. I think I was supposed to have taken detailed notes on Dr V's instructions. Somehow I'd missed my opportunity. All that was on the paper was a small misshapen snowman bearing what looked like a pitchfork or trident in the left hand corner and the doodle of tiny broken heart.

I lay on the bed. There were a couple of blankets but no sheets. There was also no pillowcase. I realised there was a dent in the pillow from a previous occupant's head. A few short, thick black hairs were trapped in the shallow crater which was slightly darkened by a greasy stain. I turned the pillow over to access the cleaner side and I stretched back beneath the pitiless white orb and fell asleep surprisingly quickly.

There was a faint knock on the door.

I felt really groggy and I didn't respond. I heard the key being slotted into the lock and Miss A opened the door.

I had no watch and really had no idea of the time. I guessed it was evening but in fact it could have been any time.

She still seemed a little irritated by me although I don't know why.

She opened a neat little case. I could see that it contained clothes and useful items that I would never have thought of packing, such as a toothbrush and even a neat little coil of dental floss with a discrete knot in it to maintain its form.

'I'm in real trouble if anyone finds out I've done this. I could only do this because the security cameras are down at the moment.'

I thanked her and sat a little forlornly on the edge of the bed.

I meant to ask her what time it was but I forgot.

'You've got to take this seriously. You have to be fully prepared for tomorrow. There's no room for mistakes and no second chance.'

I was unable to admit that I didn't know what she was talking about.

'You'll be brought breakfast early tomorrow morning. Then I'll take you down so that you can make a start. You've got to be ready. They're not on your side. Don't ever think that. That's why it's like this.'

I think she was referring to the derelict nature of everything.

She left the room and locked the door again.

No kiss then. Not even a peck on the cheek.

I followed the instructions and put the ready-made meal in the microwave. When it pinged I sat at the table and consumed it with the white plastic fork provided.

I removed my shirt and trousers.

I still had no idea of the time. I searched the case that Miss A had brought me but there was no clock. There was nothing to do but sleep.

The light switch was high up on the wall. I flicked it up and down several times but the light remained on.

I lay back on the bed in my vest and underpants and tried to sleep again beneath the harsh light. Since I'd been asleep earlier this was much harder to do and the light started to drive me mad. At one point I stood on the chair and wondered if I could remove the glass orb and take the bulb out. There was no sign of how it was fixed on. I wondered if it screwed off but when I touched the glass it was hot. Even if I managed to get the orb off, I envisaged difficulty in handling the bulb. I imagined accidentally dropping it so that it shattered on the floor, thus plunging me into incurable darkness. Or even if I'd been able to successfully remove the bulb I would probably be unable to relocate it when I needed light again.

I seemed to be living between extreme possibilities:

Absolute darkness or perpetual light.

Which was worse? In the end I opted for perpetual light. It seemed safest.

I slept intermittently.

At some indeterminate point in time there was a knock at the door. This time I was awake. I shouted for the person to come in. I expected it would be Miss A. I heard the door being unlocked but nobody entered. I shouted again to come in but nothing happened. I went to the door and opened it. There was a tray on the floor outside bearing a minimal breakfast.

Still in my vest and underpants I peeked up and down the corridor. Nobody was there. There was no natural light in the corridor either. For all I knew it was still the middle of the night.

I brought the tray in and sat down at the table.

It consisted of croissant, no butter and a little section of cheese spread in a foil wrapper but the label had been removed. There was a large mug of black coffee, one of those little round plastic containers of UHT cream and a couple of sachets of white sugar. The cream hardly penetrated the murk of the coffee. I split the croissant and it virtually shattered when I applied the cheese spread. An avalanche of fragments cascaded across the table when I attempted mastication.

When I was drinking the coffee there was another knock at the door.

This time it was Miss A. I was still in my vest and underpants. She seemed oblivious. She told me urgently that I had to come now. She walked off immediately. I left half the coffee and quickly pulled on my shirt and trousers and grabbed my jacket. With shoes untied I left the room.

Miss A was waiting at the end of the corridor.

She looked disapproving.

'I did provide you with a razor.'

I must have looked a bit rough.

'And a comb.'

'I didn't have a clock and I had no idea what time it was. I couldn't switch the light out. So I didn't sleep too well.'

She didn't say anything more.

'I don't suppose you can give me some means of telling the time?

She continued to ignore me.

We went through countless corridors and up several flights of stairs. I realised there was no natural light anywhere. For all I knew we might have been going in circles, in order that I remained ignorant of the geography of the building.

Eventually we stopped at blue double doors with glass reinforced by a grid of wire.

I could see beyond. There was an orderly standing beside a table. His face was virtually hidden by a mask and a blue cap.

'Put this gown on. When you enter the room you must not speak to the orderly. He will simply leave and let you get on with it. The ventilation is down. You will need this.'

She handed me a mask.

'In fact pretty well everything is down. But there is a purpose to everything. Remember that. You will stop for a lunch break at one o clock. You will have half an hour. I will come and see you back to your room.'

She put on a mask and we went through the doors.

The orderly immediately left and Miss A gestured to the table in the middle of the room.

There was a sheet covering an inert mass.

I stood unresponding. Miss A gestured again.

Despite the mask, things didn't smell too good. I could see there were feet in rather nice shoes sticking out at one end, so I went to the other. I did feel a sense of dread.

I pulled the blanket back.

Despite the trace of green and a modicum of bloating which stretched the skin and reduced the apparent age, even I recognised who it was. The ear to ear grin was the giveaway.

'But isn't that~ '

I'm terrible with names.

Miss A seemed exasperated.

'Who did you expect? You really haven't been following any of this have you?'

I still couldn't put a name to the face.

'Haven't you been following the news? You've got Tony Blair.'

No, I never follow the news.

Even in death he looked surprisingly good. Better than most in fact. Certainly better than one would have imagined.

Miss A seemed less impressed.

'Well, he hasn't exactly achieved odeur de sainteté has he? I'll leave you to it.'

But leave me to what exactly?

I wasn't very happy.

I found I was only comfortable when my eyes were averted from the body.

It's hard to explain but it was a bit disturbing.

I examined the immediate proximity. There was a little cabinet with a scattering of instruments in the drawer. There was a lamp. The floor had shiny tiles with drains in the corner covered with metal grids. I suspected that when I had finished the room would be hosed down and scrubbed clean. All discarded remnants and fluids would be permanently washed away.

There was a sink in the corner. It had ordinary taps, not the fancy ones that you see surgeons scrubbing up with on the television that they operate with their elbows. I tried them. Oddly there was hot water but no cold. When I turned on the cold tap it made the whispering noise of pale ghosts but nothing came out. On the other hand scalding water came from the hot tap. It came out in angry, spasmodic splutters suggesting that the source supplying it was actually boiling. It felt unstable as if something was about to rupture, so I turned it off.

The window was covered with a white slatted blind. I tweaked the slats apart and found once again that the actual window was bricked up.

Next to the window there was an extractor fan. It didn't seem to be on. I pressed the switch several times but nothing happened.

It's funny how you can pass the time in situations like this (not that I'd actually been in this situation before). I wandered up and down, then round and round the room.

There was a surveillance camera high up on the wall but I couldn't tell if it was on. It certainly didn't follow me about even though it appeared to have the appropriate mechanisms.

I finally returned to Mr Blair. Oddly I was disturbed by how still he was. He literally hadn't moved a muscle. But then wasn't he dead?

I noticed there was a dossier on top of the cabinet of instruments.

I picked it up and realised that it was a full report of the circumstances of the terrorist atrocity that had killed Mr

Blair and several other people. I thought I had better read it. That's a good start.

Far from being a fascinating read it turned out to be highly detailed and written in a dense technical language. Involuntarily I found myself beginning to skip paragraphs. All I can remember for certain was that it was 658 pages long. Or was it 685 pages?

The skipping of paragraphs quickly changed to the skipping of pages. In the end I just flicked through the remainder all the way to the end.

I put it down.

I had that feeling of deep boredom welling up from my stomach. I couldn't latch on to any information.

I thought I'd better try harder with the dossier. I had another go, but the same thing happened again except quicker.

I had no idea what time it was but I prayed it would be lunchtime soon.

It felt like another two or three hours passed before Miss A returned. When she did return I felt intense relief.

'You don't seem to have made much progress.'

'I was reading the dossier.'

'Good. You got through it all.'

'Yes.'

'If you've finished it I have instructions to remove it.'

I think I looked a bit uncomfortable.

'You have read it? This is important. You haven't just idled the morning away?

'I think I read the relevant bits.'

'Right.'

I know I'm doing it again. I'm just telling her what she hopes to be the case.

She picked up the dossier and put it beneath her arm.

'I'll take you back for lunch.'

As we left the room the orderly returned apparently to watch over Mr Blair.

As we walked back along the corridors I felt I ought to come clean that I hadn't actually read the dossier but I couldn't make myself. I also meant to reiterate that I had no means to tell the time but I felt similarly impeded.

Miss A unlocked the door. I hope she would come in with me and that maybe we could pass a little time together. But as soon as I stepped inside, the door behind me shut and locked.

Lunch was waiting on the table.

It consisted of a cup of instant soup and a Pot Noodle, both with the hot water already added. How did they know my accustomed eating habits? I was impressed. Although I could have done with another cup of coffee, foul though it was, but they seemed to assume that the soup sufficed for liquid refreshment.

Somehow I didn't feel that hungry. I popped the soup in the microwave.

The end result was that I drank all the soup but left a third of the Pot Noodle.

I remember I hadn't shaved. I looked in the bag that Miss A had given me. I hoped for a small electric razor. Instead there was shaving foam and single disposable razor. I made myself reasonably presentable.

I took the opportunity to evacuate my bowels. At least I attempted to. I sat on the misplaced toilet and waited, but my intestinal track seemed unwilling to cooperate. Like a small child I put on a grimace of concentration, eyes tightly closed and made a grunting sound as I strained harder.

Miss A walked in. With my trousers round my ankles I did my best to assume a posture of dignity.

Miss A seemed unsurprised and unimpressed. How romantic it was all turning out.

'You must come now. I'll give you two minutes to sort yourself out.'

Exactly two minutes later she returned. This time I was reasonably presentable but the bowel evacuation had been a failure.

I didn't even manage to urinate.

We didn't speak at all during the return journey.

I started to worry that I'd lied about reading the dossier. It plagued my thoughts that I should come clean about it and ask for it back. I felt inhibited to actually mention it.

When we returned to the autopsy room the orderly was still standing next to Mr Blair. The blanket had been replaced. The orderly was no longer wearing a mask or cap.

He was quite overweight with a shaven head with what looked like a malignant mole spreading from the top. He'd missed quite a lot of hairs in his shaving routine and they'd grown quite long.

'Well, he hasn't walked off. He's all yours again.'

He seemed very pleasant and friendly. This made a refreshing change.

I was just about to open my mouth and reply but Miss A grabbed my arm and pulled me to the side.

'Do not exchange pleasantries.'

She was quite sharp.

I started to wonder if I did in fact like her. Maybe this wasn't going to turn out to be a marriage made in heaven after all.

'But he does seem quite a nice chap. At least he's turning out to be friendly. It's quite a rare commodity around here.'

'They're trying to make you break protocol. It's a deliberate ploy.'

I went off in a bit of sulk.

Miss A and the orderly departed and once again I was alone with Mr Blair.

As I mentioned, the cover had been replaced over Mr Blair. In order to show willing I pulled it aside again.

I suddenly noticed that the room was extremely warm. This seemed to contradict any aim to preserve Mr Blair in any reasonable condition.

This did not bode well.

For the first time I noticed that Mr Blair was still fully clothed. There didn't seem to be any damage to the suit he was wearing. Surely some important inference was to be drawn from this but I couldn't for the life of me think what it was.

I felt that it was a good start to remove the clothes.

I started with the shoes.

They were those really expensive ones made of soft leather. They contrasted somewhat with my desert boots. I was possessed of a huge urge to try them on.

They were a little too big but so much more comfortable than my own.

I left my own shoes underneath the trolley and walked about a bit. They felt really good.

I turned my attention to the security camera.

I climbed up on a chair and had a really good look. I could see that a red wire was dangling from the back. I felt fairly confident that it wasn't working. Nobody was watching me. Maybe there wasn't that much to worry about, at least at this point in time.

I clambered back down.

I suddenly wondered if the light switch worked.

I flipped it down and was plunged immediately into absolute darkness. Usually there is some glimmer of light from somewhere but there was none. I'd already noted the windows had been bricked up.

I made the mistake of moving away from the light switch and in the heat and stench of decay I became disorientated. I was several steps into the room but I couldn't find my way back to the light switch.

I found the table. I put my hand out but I couldn't locate Mr Blair. I had the curious sense that he was floating above in the darkness somewhere, born by the gases of putrefaction.

I reached up as high as I could but I could find nothing.

I felt giddy and swimmy and my feet seemed to have left the floor. I had the sense we were both orbiting the room as if we were performing synchronised swimming in a slow stately motion.

Hours passed but I was unable to escape the predicament.

Suddenly my eyes were stabbed with light flooding into the room.

Miss A was standing by the light switch looking at me with stark disapproval.

'You've been asleep.'

'He's gone. I don't know where he is.'

'You've been asleep. He's there on the trolley where he's been all along. Have you been looking for him long?'

She was right. Mr Blair was still on the trolley.

'You haven't even taken the cover off.'

'I have.'

But it was apparent that I hadn't.

The chair that I'd stood on to examine the surveillance camera was behind me lying on its side. I could see that it created the impression that I'd been asleep sitting in the chair and that when Miss A switched on the light I'd stood up suddenly and knocked over the chair.

Confused, I put my hand on my forehead.

I could feel a deep straight dent going across my forehead as if it had been resting on the edge of the trolley for some time and had left an imprint. The corner of my mouth was moist with an accumulation of saliva.

'We've got to go.'

I seemed unable to respond.

'Now.'

I followed Miss A along the corridors back to my room. She left me at the door.

'If you don't buck your ideas up soon, then God help you.'

The door slammed shut.

I looked down at my feet. I was still wearing Mr Blair's shoes. I also realised that, inexplicably, I was also wearing his trousers. I wondered what had happened to my clothes.

This looked bad. I had to remember to change them back tomorrow.

There was another ready-made meal in the microwave. Again there was a small green, very sour apple but in better condition than the last.

This time there was no banana.

Sleeping was as poor and intermittent as it had been on the previous night.

Maybe I had been asleep all afternoon. But again, I couldn't sleep now under the harsh light. I covered my head with my jumper and entered a state in which I was neither awake or asleep.

The breakfast routine with croissant and section of cheese spread was repeated. This time I left the croissant but drank almost half of the coffee.

I spent most of the time trying to evacuate my bowels. It needed to be done before Miss A appeared. Once again I failed miserably.

Miss A arrived to collect me.

As we walked through the corridors some sort of difference must have struck me although it was hard to specify exactly what it was.

'We're not going the usual way.'

'No, we're going to the Resource Centre. You've got to start making a proper effort. Instead of pissing your time away you can find out what you're supposed to be doing.'

I looked down at my feet. I was still wearing Mr Blair's shoes. This didn't look good. The trousers were more or less covered by the gown that I'd been wearing since yesterday morning. But the shoes seemed a bit of a giveaway. I didn't feel I could mention this to Miss A. I was in trouble enough as it was.

We went through the automatic doors to a reception desk.

The bloke had a close-trimmed authoritarian beard.

He asked to see my security pass.

I opened up my gown and allowed him access. He leant forward with the sort of hand-held scanners they sometimes use in shops and glanced at his computer screen.

'Category One?'

I nodded.

The fact that his expression remained exactly the same seemed to speak volumes, unfortunately the volumes continued to be written in a language that I was unable to discern.

Far up the corridor, through the automatic door, I think I glimpsed Dr V disappearing through a door.

I started to think that Miss A had timed things rather well.

The main body of the Resource Centre was completely empty. The entire building appeared to be scantly populated.

Miss A had a busy schedule planned.

She sat down at a computer terminal and started clicking buttons.

'Right you've read the dossier detailing the crime scene, the immediate condition of the body, the ambient temperature etc. You can see straight away they are not following the standard protocol despite what they may say. The body hasn't been adequately refrigerated. There are no assistants such as prosectors to attend the internal organs.

There isn't even a forensic photographer. Where is the mortuary technician? They haven't even removed the clothes.'

I stood immediately behind her trying to make it so that she couldn't see my shoes.

'You have to stay ahead of their game.'

The printer beneath the terminal started to issue stacks of printed pages.

'You need to take samples from the body for examination. Samples sent to histology lab reveal information about the tissues and cells. Toxicology deals with toxins, poisons etc.

She started to hand me the printed pages.

'It's all here. Don't muddle them up.'

As soon as she removed one pile of papers from the printer another immediately started to gather.

'You've got to make a Y incision. You've got to make an incision through the skin, starting at the chest and reaching to both shoulders. Then from the chest down to the pubic bone. You've got to pull the skin back and reveal the ribcage. Then you've got to remove the front of the ribcage so that you can access the heart and other organs.'

'How?'

'The equipment must be there. You probably use a saw or some cutting device. You have to discern whether the organs have been damaged and whether that damage was the primary cause of death.'

She was interrupted by a paging device, attached to her wrist, signalling an alert. For a couple of seconds she studied the device.

'I've got to go now. I've no more time. What do you want to do? You can stay here and get more information or you can return to the autopsy room. It's up to you.'

I couldn't decide.

'Quickly.'

'I'll go back to the autopsy room.'

I trotted after her, piled up with printed pages up to my chin trying not to drop any of them.

'If anybody finds out I've helped you then we're both in trouble. Time's running out. Read the stuff I've given you and for God's sake get on with it.'

As soon as we got there she departed at some speed.

Before anything else happened I had to change the shoes and trousers back. I let the pages drop into a disordered heap on the floor and I removed the sheet from Mr Blair's body.

He was wearing not only my shoes and trousers but the rest of my clothes.

They were a little tight on him and looked a bit scruffy.

I peeked beneath my gown and found that I was wearing Mr Blair's suit. A further examination revealed my white, ragged M&S Y-fronts had been replaced by considerably smarter, blue-striped Calvin Kline boxer shorts with a black waistband.

I was no longer wearing my vest. Applying the same logic I sort of assumed that in turn Mr Blair was wearing my vest and pants.

I caught a glimpse of myself in the glass of the door wearing Mr Blair's suit. It revealed an unattainable version of myself.

But I couldn't work out how any of this had happened. But then I am a bit depleted and sleep deprived.

I began the task of changing back. Miss A's conduct had alerted in me a small panic that I had to get something done. That time might be running out. I started to have a feeling that something unpleasant was about to happen. I really could have done without this.

When Miss A returned for the lunch break at least I had managed to get my old clothes back on.

Once again she seemed exasperated.

'You haven't managed to get his clothes off then?'

Then I realised my next mistake.

As well as my own, I had replaced all Mr Blair's clothes.

Anybody reading my confession will realise that, at this point, I was beginning to lose it a bit. I completely lost track of the sessions in the autopsy room.

I also lost count as to how many days I'd been there.

I would go back expecting the cup of instant soup and Pot Noodle but instead found a microwave meal and a mouldering banana.

I muddled day and night completely.

Sometimes it seemed that after Miss A delivered me to the autopsy room, no more than five minutes past before she arrived to return me to my room. However, she constantly denied this and accused me of falling asleep. But then I was rarely able to sleep in my room when I was supposed to. Maybe she was right.

Other times it seemed as if I was left in the autopsy room for days at a time.

I swear I went to bed and awoke in the dark to find myself talking in my sleep to Mr Blair. I'm certain he was talking back. But this is hard to square with the fact that it was impossible to switch off the light in my room. There was no dark in my room.

At least two more times I arrived back in my room to find myself wearing Mr Blair's clothes. In any case the shoes had become something of a fixture.

I did quite like them.

Apart from the shoes, the only definite constant in this world of flux was the absence of any bowel movement.

Finally I found myself wandering down the corridor, inexplicably unattended, and met the baldy orderly who was obviously drunk. His face came right up to mine as he pushed me against the wall. He told me that Mr Blair was 'nothing but a fruity squeezebox' before trying to plant a huge salivary kiss on my lips. Miss A turned up in the nick of time before he completely rogered me.

She squirted him with Windowlene directly into his face.

He backed away clutching at his eyes but she still blamed me for the encounter.

'How many times have I told you not to talk to him.'

She dragged me down the corridor virtually supporting my weight.

We entered the autopsy room. The floor was covered with the printed sheets that Miss A had provided me. They were crumpled and covered with footprints largely from Mr Blair's own shoes ironically. Around the table the sheets had acquired a grubby flatness as if they were gradually transforming into an impromptu carpet.

Miss A was trying to be patient with me.

'It's been days now and you still haven't removed his clothes. You haven't done anything. YOU MUST MAKE A Y-INCISION ACROSS HIS CHEST AND ABDOMEN. THIS IS THE LAST DAY. YOU MUST HAVE COMPLETED THE AUTOPSY TODAY.'

So, for the final time I was left in the autopsy room.

A little staggery and woozy perhaps but bearing up surprisingly well.

No eating, no sleeping, no shitting. But apart from that I'm fine.

I clutched onto the side of the trolley.

At least, for once, I noticed Mr Blair was back in his own clothes. A little travel worn maybe. Been round the block a few times but at least they're back in the right place.

I was still finding motivation a little tricky.

I think, when it comes down to it, that I'm a bit squeamish to touch things that are dead. A cherished pet in life becomes a shrunken object of repulsion in death.

But I did notice that Mr Blair was even more bloated than on previous occasions.

A morbid fascination supplanted my morbid disinclination.

I put my hand in the middle of his chest and pressed quite gently.

If I'm honest I'd been meaning to do this for days.

The collected gases moved from the abdomen and up through the trachea and issued through the larynx.

The lips parted and emitted a wheezing note.

Slightly repelled I stopped pressing. The note continued for a few seconds rather like bagpipes when they are placed on a table. Or an accordion for that matter. Maybe that's what the baldy, drunken orderly was talking about when he said that Blair was a squeezebox.

I pressed the chest again.

I realised that I could recognise the tone of the ex-prime minister's voice in the emission.

I started doing it over and over again, wondering if I could ever exhaust the gases of putrefaction trapped within.

I started to have the impression that there were actual words in the emission.

'…………..weapons…………..Sadd…………..'

I felt increasingly light headed. I pressed again.

'……..concludes that Iraq has chemical and biological weapons, which could be activated in 45 minutes……………'

It was a bit like playing a musical instrument. The more I practised the clearer the sound.

'The biological agents we believe Iraq can produce include anthrax, botulinum, toxin, aflatoxin and ricin. All result in an excruciating painful death.'

It didn't stop there.

'…….the Iraq Survey Group has already found massive evidence of a huge system of clandestine laboratories, workings by scientists, plans to develop long range ballistic missiles………………..'

It stopped. I tried pressing again and found that it started up louder and stronger than before.

'………we expected, I expected to find actual usable, chemical or biological weapons after we entered Iraq…………but I have to accept, as the months have passed, it seems increasingly clear that at the time of the invasion, Saddam did not have stockpiles of chemical or biological weapons ready to deploy……………'

I stopped pressing but the voice continued on its own.

'…………….and the problem is, I can apologise for the information that turned out to be wrong, but I can't, sincerely at least, apologise for removing Saddam……….'

I tried to rearrange the body to stop the sound but it wouldn't cooperate.

'……….I can only go one way, I've got no reverse gear……….'

I moved the arms out to the sides and raised one of the legs. It had no effect.

'……….I am unable to satisfy the desire even of my supporters, who would like me to say: it was a mistake but one made in good faith……..friends opposed to the war think I'm being obstinate……others, less friendly, think I'm delusional….to both I may say….keep an open mind……………..'

Nothing could make it stop. For the first time I located the communication device that had been provided to contact Miss A. I pushed the button but the battery was obviously dead.

'…………I will never know precisely what made Dr David Kelly take his own life. Who can ever know the reason behind those things? It was so sad, unnecessary and terrible……………'

I ran to the door.

'…………I had come to like and admire George. I was asked recently which of the political leaders I had met had the most integrity. I listed George near the top. Some people were aghast……thinking I was joking. He had genuine integrity and as much political courage as any leader I have ever met. He was, in a bizarre sense……a true idealist……………………….'

The door wouldn't open. I started to beat my fist against the glass.

I screamed to be let out. Beyond the glass door the building seemed to be entirely deserted.

'…………..do they really suppose I don't care, don't feel, don't regret with every fibre of my being the loss of those who died? To be indifferent to that would be inhuman, emotionally warped………………'

I ripped open the cabinet next to the trolley and selected the implement most resembling a stout knife.

With a savage cry, I stabbed down as hard as I could into the middle of his chest.

Warm blood projected by a heartbeat flowed over my hand.

Mr Blair sat up and screamed. He grabbed at my collar and pulled himself close to my face.

'What have you done?'

He fell back down. I was still holding the knife and as he writhed it came away in my hand.

I'd spoiled his suit. It was covered in blood.

An alarm sounded behind me. The lights started to flash on and off.

There was a brief pause before the room filled with armed police wearing protective visors.

They threw me to the ground and several guns pointed at my head. As I was dragged out, in the confusion, I could just make out a medical team descending on Mr Blair.

I was stood up against the wall immediately outside the autopsy room. The knife was still in my hand and I was aware that I was covered in blood.

I noticed the alarm had been switched off but the activity was massive.

A very tall officer in an almost kindly way said they wanted to take a few photographs.

'We don't want another Barry George do we?'

A camera flashed several times.

The knife was taken from me by a hand in rubber clothes and placed in a plastic bag and carefully sealed. Another tall officer almost indistinguishable from the first started to explain the procedure.

'I'm sorry but we are required to do this.'

Several officers took me into the corner and proceeded to kick and punch me in the face and stomach.

I tasted blood in my mouth and promptly folded up on the floor.

I was a bit winded. I lay there for a few minutes then strong hands raised me to my feet. I was aware that I was still wearing Mr Blair's shoes but the trousers were my own.

'We are following a strict protocol. We are required to demonstrate some emotion at the assassination of a respected leader but it is essential that the extent of the emotion is sufficiently restrained so as to be in keeping with standards expected of an organisation that sustains the rule of law. We are, after all, a median civilised country. We consider the assassination of Indira Gandhi to be botched because the assailants surrendered, but both were still shot, one of them killed. At the very least we can't be seen to encourage sympathy among the supporters of the assassin. We adopt the American model following the assassination of President Kennedy. The assassin was beaten during the arrest but kept alive. The rest is history, of course. It was the best thing for the assassin. It always is. But from the start it wasn't going to be your lucky day.'

It was all surprisingly cordial. I'd got my breath back and for some reason felt it was appropriate to join in the conversation.

'I haven't had a shit for days.'

'That's the least of your problems.'

I was handcuffed and led out of the building.

It turned out to be a rather pleasant spring morning. Quite early on I'd lost all sense as to which season it was.

As I was loaded into a van I could see Dr V in the distance walking towards a car. Miss A was following close behind carrying a stack of papers. They seemed a little stained and dog eared. I think they were the one's I'd left scattered on the floor of the autopsy room. She held them down as the breeze lifted some of the corners of pages.

Just before the doors of the van were closed, Miss A briefly turned to look at me.

Well, at least I thought she did.

The Conclusion of the Final Conference of the 'Seventh Extinction'.

A clinical, female voice delivered a message on the tannoy.

'A polar bear has been spotted in the vicinity of the university. Emergency measures are being put into place immediately.'

I was waiting in the foyer of the university theatre with a subdued crowd. Following the delivery of the message I could clearly detect the tension. Metal shutters loudly clattered over the windows and entrance. For a few seconds we were left in almost perfect darkness before the lighting came on. As if to reinforce the tension, almost immediately the lights went out. For a few seconds they flickered on again but somewhat dimmer than before, then they went altogether.

Nobody spoke or moved. The emergency lighting kicked in producing a general issue of relief. The glow was a bit minimal but adequate. The shadows were now well pronounced. It definitely added to the atmosphere of menace.

I decided it was a good time to take a cigarette break.

I glanced across to a group of emaciated PhD students who'd caught a whiff of smoke and were looking at me with resentment and distaste.

I thought I'd better get a dialogue going.

'I know all these security measures have kicked in for good reason but it seems ironic that they probably contravene every safety regulation. I mean, if a fire was to break out now how on earth would we all leave the building?'

One of them snorted.

A security guard came up to me.

'There's a strict rule of no smoking. I'm afraid you must put that out immediately.'

I usually do as I'm told. I dropped the cigarette and extinguished it under my shoe. To please the disapproving students I gave it an extra twist to make sure there was no spark remaining and that the tobacco was dispersed beyond all reasonable doubt. At least we were now protected against fire.

I continued my conversation with the students as if I was completely oblivious of their moral disapproval.

'There must be something big going on out there if the power has gone. Something really, really big trying to get in. I wonder how long we're going to be able to keep it out.'

Nobody wanted to join in so I was forced to continue on my own.

'I mean, I wonder how things will go. Will you be able to go home after the conference? Just a matter of hanging about for a while. Or is that going to be it? The end. No more anything.'

I got the impression that they didn't like me very much. Not really one of their kind I suppose. A couple of the nearer students turned their shoulders towards me as if to exclude me and change the conversation. But no conversation ensued.

They know perfectly well who I am. I may not have any first class honours degrees but they know that until recently I was Professor Rowtley's right hand man. They must have been aware that it was me that was whispering in Professor Rowtley's ear during the legendary, if somewhat acerbic, debates with Professor Rauls pertaining to the role of mankind (whoops, sorry ladies) -I mean humankind in nature. It was two grand old men of science collapsing into the emeritus phase of their academic careers. Raul's wasn't doing too badly on the whole but Professor Rowtley was definitely in need of prompting. A little bit of shaping and modulation here and there. The liver spots on the head weren't there for nothing.

Professor Rauls argued the tired, poncy liberal dictum that the only creature on the planet of worth in itself was of the rational variety now congregated in the foyer of the university theatre (in fact all that is probably left now). The rest of creation had no value other than as a means of providing succour and recreation for the privileged race (dare I call it the Master Race?). To back up his argument he imagined the situation in which the human race faced imminent extinction (let us call this the seventh extinction for reasons that will become clear later on) and that there remained just one last man (oops, sorry again ladies) –I mean there remained one last person. Professor Rauls insisted that clearly, if that person's last act was to obliterate the planet and all who sail in her, then no real damage would be done.

Professor Rowtley cleverly countered this conclusion, making the highly effective argument (thanks to me) to the effect that Professor Raul's last person was basically a bit of shit and that we should try to be a bit more considerate to our fellow plants and animals.

Of course, as always in these situations no side wins outright.

As they say, the debate goes on, but as it turned out, not for much longer.

The doors to the lecture theatre opened and the subdued gathering filtered in.

The lecture theatre is quite large. The majority of seats are contained in the main central column. Aisles separate the central column from two smaller columns either side. Most people sat in the middle. I sat right at the back distanced by several rows.

Five or six people were scattered in the outside columns.

Only a few weeks ago Professor Rowtley had the pulling power to completely fill the theatre (but maybe the population is beginning to thin out a bit).

I found that if I shielded my eyes with my hands and excluded the peripheries I could create the illusion (at least to myself) that the lecture theatre was almost full.

When I removed my hands, the outside columns were now completely empty.

Professor Rowtley came in five minutes after the lecture was due to start.

He put a wad of papers on the table and began to speak.

I cut across him.

'Given the statement over the tannoy a few moments ago, can the professor assure us that we are completely safe in here and that the polar bear presents no further threat?'

Heads were twisting round to locate the voice.

'Given the present political/evolutional predicament, I'm afraid that I cannot make such a guarantee.'

I noticed that the 'post-relativity Einstein' hairdo, which long spoke of the demise of the productive phase of academic life, was beginning to unravel. The pale, pink scalp of a little old man was now peeping through (I don't need to mention the liver spots again).

When I spoke he gave no sign whatsoever that he recognised me. He's still capable of displaying that sort of professional discretion.

'I must point out that the security service has actually recommended that the theatre door behind me be locked. It could be a mistake but I have agreed to this measure.'

He began his address.

'All of you who have followed the debate between Professor Rauls and myself over recent years will be aware that we were coming to what might be termed an unhappy reconciliation. Professor Rauls was supposed to attend this final lecture in the conference on the seventh extinction but

I'm sorry to inform you that Professor Rauls was assassinated, in his home, just before he set out for this meeting. Obviously we will sorely miss his final views on the seventh extinction. Beyond our academic differences we were always close friends.'

I don't think too many people noticed my snort.

I must admit he did look a bit shaken but he did a good job of carrying on.

'The first five extinctions have been well documented in our natural history. These were simply natural catastrophes.

'The first, as you probably know was the 'Ordovician-Silurian' extinction. Basically it was an overextended ice age that destroyed roughly 85% of species of marine life over, roughly, ten million years.

'Then there was the extinction in the late Devonian caused by a reduction of oxygen in the atmosphere termed 'anoxia'. This lasted 25 million years during which three quarters of species, both marine and terrestrial, vanished.

'The third extinction, the 'Permian-Triasic' removed 95% of species. This was down to a combination of factors. Anoxia, volcanic activity and maybe several asteroid impacts. This was relatively brief, lasting approximately 100,000 years.

'Then there was the 'Triassic-Jurassic' extinction. It lasted only 10,000 years but 90% of species disappeared. Again this was a combination of effects, namely extreme climate change, asteroid impacts and volcanic activity.

'The fifth extinction, the one everybody knows, was the 'Cretaceous-Tertiary' that brought an end to the dinosaurs. The most likely cause was massive impacts of asteroids.

'This leads us to the sixth extinction which is solely down to man's intrusive activity on the planet. It began with the advent of modern man and has accelerated since. The main causes are the destruction of natural habitats, the introduction of alien species, pollution, over-exploitation of species for consumption, monoculture, human induced climate change, the acidification of the oceans due to climate change etc, etc.'

Professor Rowtley paused and surveyed the room.

'Professor, you haven't mentioned the melting of the polar icecaps. Is this of any concern?'

I wondered if he had noticed that, despite the door being locked, the audience had thinned somewhat since the start of the lecture. I think I've already mentioned the disappearances at the peripheries (but who cares about the margins anyway?) But since then I reckon that the population in the middle block has declined by about a half. There was definitely no longer any sign of the PhD students that I had encountered earlier (no great loss I would guess).

'I mean, what about the effect of the polar bears, professor?'

Professor Rowtley rebuffed me well, in order to maintain his authority over the lecture.

'I'm about to come on to that point. And I hope there will be time at the end for questions. So if you wait to make your comments we will be able to get through the subject matter all the quicker.'

I doubted that there would be much time at the end for questions.

'The prospect of the seventh extinction has been puzzling us for a while. This, of course, refers to the coming extinction of humankind itself, the perpetrator of the previous extinction. It seems that certain species, on the verge of extinction, mainly the polar bears we suspect, have made an unprecedented evolutionary recovery. Through natural selection their form, for want of a better word, has radically altered beyond all recognition. This change puts to question our fundamental understanding of biology and maybe the underlying physics as well. Basically the polar bears are back and they're coming for us with a vengeance.'

I refused to keep quiet.

'Professor Rowtley, can you provide us with more details of Professor Rauls tragic demise?'

It was a fair question, I needed more clarity but Professor Rowtley seemed reluctant.

'You mentioned he was assassinated, professor. That has quite a strong implication. I mean it rules out natural causes. Clearly it wasn't a heart attack or some sort of haemorrhage. Presumably not an accident of any kind. Was he actually eaten by a wild animal, Professor Rowtley?'

'I think you know the answer to that one.'

I feel vindicated. You see, he does know who I am.

'But how can being eaten by a wild animal constitute an assassination, Professor? Doesn't that imply the perpetrator was in the control of a rational agent, or was even a rational agent itself?'

Professor Rowtley decided to ignore my question and push on with his lecture. Looking back I think that was a good idea. Time was definitely beginning to press.

'As you all know over the last few weeks there has been a rapid exponential diminution of the world's human population. It has been halving with unprecedented rapidity. In the chaos resulting, the cause has not been identified.'

'Is this what is happening inside this very lecture theatre, Professor Rowtley?'

It certainly was a bit alarming. There were now only three or four of us left.

'When is the deadline, Professor Rowtley? When does it all end? There must be a prediction.'

'There hasn't been sufficient data available.'

'Oh come on Professor. Make a stab. The tabloids are claiming that it's all going to end for us today at about midday. That coincides roughly with the completion of this conference, that is, if it all runs to schedule.'

Professor Rowtley refused to be drawn.

But maybe there was little point. Everyone else has gone now.

It's just me and the Professor.

'So, Professor. Who goes next? Me or you? It's fifty-fifty as to which one. Which will it be?'

'You know the answer.'

I must admit the Professor is remaining astonishingly cool and calm.

'What are your final thoughts then Professor Rowtley? If Professor Rauls had lived to attend the final debate, what was going to happen? What was the conclusion to be? Are the rumours true that you've shifted your position closer to Professor Rauls? Originally you thought Professor Rauls' last man was a bit of a shit and that he should have tried to be a bit nicer (I'm sorry ladies, but it is all down to blokes if we're being honest -you don't really get a look in do you?). But that seems to describe your predicament now, Professor. Maybe you're now thinking that the last man simply wasn't a big enough shit to cope with the changing world?'

But as they say all that's academic now.

Professor Rowtley has gone.

Never to return.

I left the empty auditorium (the locked door presented no problem).

I put on my sunglasses in the bright sunshine and strolled down the empty street. It is warmer than I'm used to, but I can get used to it.

Suddenly the world seemed pleasant and renewed.

A Bird of Dereliction

We learn the most peculiar facts about ourselves at the oddest times.

Not more than two days ago, shortly after supper, I sneezed.

Hardly a remarkable incident in itself.

The sneeze appeared to have no cause. No cause at least in the sense that I wasn't starting a cold, I'm not a hay fever sufferer (besides it's the middle of winter) and there hadn't been an event which might have resulted in the dislodging of dust and may have acted as an irritant.

The cause was subtle, yet the sneeze was large. So large in fact that my false teeth shot from my mouth.

And there lies the peculiarity.

As far as I was concerned I had never worn false teeth. As far as I knew I didn't need to wear false teeth since my natural teeth appeared to be in a fit state, stationed correctly in their positions in the upper and lower jaw.

The item that lay before me on the carpet, top and bottom plate, still clenched, was a source of complete surprise.

When the first sense of shock passed, I assumed somebody was playing a joke on me.

Gingerly, as if I half expected an unprovoked attack of biting, snarling and spitting, I picked the teeth up and carefully examined them.

They certainly had the appearance of the teeth that I was long familiar with. I recognised their irregularities, their colour, even the fillings were present. I could clearly make out fibres of chicken from the Indian take-away I'd devoured as a near starving man an hour ago.

Time to make an internal check.

I probed with my tongue the quadrants of my mouth. North. South. East. West.

It was true. A deserted cavern of raw gum. The once over-crowded space within was definitely empty.

It was hard to leave it at that. Just pop them back inside as if nothing had happened, live my life to the end of my days without a further thought on the incident.

It's times like these that you need your loved one beside you. Unfortunately my wife, Tina, was busy at a conference, proposing that the seat of the male soul is situated at the tip of the penis, whereas the female soul is firmly placed amidst the higher cognitive functions that generate humanitarian concern.

Straightaway, in front of the mirror, I could see that my face had changed shape. Obviously a vital part of the skeletal support had gone astray and a whole new range of possibilities opened up for facial expressions formally beyond the scope of my abilities.

I must admit, I felt a sense of insecurity.

Was my hair about to slide off my head, turning out to be a toupee?

A wooden leg to clatter unexpectedly onto the floor?

I believe I sat staring at the teeth for an hour trying to decide what to do. I came to no conclusions.

I collected a glass of water from the kitchen and watched, with sadness, the teeth drift to the bottom like a clenched mussel sinking in an unfamiliar ocean. Carrying the glass, I tramped up the stairs and climbed straight into bed. Suddenly there was no need for the old routines anymore. Certainly no need to clean the teeth. I placed the dentures on the bedside table and turned my back to them.

Must remember to buy Steradent tomorrow.

More importantly I needed to see a dentist.

If only this problem had been in isolation.

But unfortunately not. Strange things had been happening for some time. For instance there was the disappearance of my wife's breasts. This coincided with the reversion of my penis to its childhood status. The latter was closely related to the former and the former was related to the birth of our son Thomas.

Thomas was a greedy baby and as well as drinking every drop of milk, somehow managed to gobble up the substance of the breast tissue. Certainly by the time that Thomas had finished with my wife's breasts they had virtually shrunk to nothing, as well as leaving them oddly distorted.

I know that I should not admit this, but my wife's breasts were her most profound feature. In the first place, their presence provided the vital catalyst in the formation of our relationship that, to many, happened when we were both too young. They were the flowers in the garden of our romance. They protruded into my fancies and pressed warmly into the sweaty dreams occurring in the nights of late adolescence.

So where is my wife now?

Indeed, where is the seat of the male soul?

Certainly the seat of my soul has shrunk miserably and presumably likewise the soul encased within.

I would have hoped, indeed prayed, that my wife's first duty was to the restoration of her breasts to their former glory.

But no.

She turned instead to cerebral matters.

Things began to rub a bit at this stage. We'd both left school without any useful qualifications. Then suddenly, during Thomas's infancy, at the exact instance of the final disappearance of her breasts, my wife simultaneously discovered her cerebral cortex and feminism.

A library appeared from nothing in our living room. Correspondence courses came and went with spectacular results. She acquired a disgustingly splendid degree and I began to realise that I was being left behind. Post graduate studies ensued and any reasonable chance of a return of the breasts, as I remembered them so long ago, became hopeless.

Finally, there was the mysterious re-emergence of Roy into an uncharted hinterland of our marriage that denied me any right of access.

When I awoke in the morning I realised that it was to Roy that I needed to turn for help.

The main difficulty behind doing anything about the problem with my teeth is that I don't regularly attend a dentist. In fact I haven't seen a dentist for years and years.

Roy was a dentist.

He was, first, my closest childhood friend and later, a rival in love with Tina, in our late adolescence. The better man lost. I believe Tina felt slightly intimidated by Roy as well as fancying him more than me. He possessed ambition and direction. I lacked both of these. As my relationship with Tina developed, Roy disappeared to the realms of higher education.

I heard he'd come back as a dentist and I knew where he practised, although I hadn't seen him for years. I knew that he was more successful than me and that Tina had been seeing him recently. Tina assured me that she was only collaborating with Roy in a project to determine the links between orthodontic correction and male sexual perversions.

I had to forget all that for the moment. It was as a friend that I needed Roy at the moment.

The next morning I plucked the teeth from their watery grave and popped them back in my mouth and then phoned Roy's practise to beg to see him. The receptionist was difficult about the matter. She appeared to disbelieve me about the problem with the teeth, obviously thinking that I needed psychiatric help. I managed to persuade her that Roy was an old friend and that I must speak to him. To prove the friendship I started to babble the details of our mutual

childhood. Halfway through a cool male voice started to
speak.

"I suppose there are one or two important things we
must clear up. Look I'll come round this evening after I've
finished surgery. Just after seven?"

I was certainly impressed with Roy. Without knowing
any of the details about my teeth, his profound, analytic
dentist's brain had anticipated my problem and was already
processing possible solutions. Shortly after seven o clock, just
as I was slicing pieces of ham, the doorbell rang. I opened the
door to receive Roy. Although he obviously looked older I
could still see the small boy, like an unexorcised ghost, trapped
in a prison of fine lines.

Still holding the kitchen knife from my sandwich-
making activities, I waved him into the living room. Roy
looked awkward and immediately opened his mouth to speak.
Suddenly I felt a surge of affection for him and felt pleased to
see him. Before he could utter I butted in.

"Something to drink? Refreshments? What about
Murden's pop, seven pence a bottle with three pence back on
the bottle leaving us just enough money to buy a packet of
Smith's crisps with the salt wrapped up in a little square of
blue paper? We can drink to the Saturdays of childhood."

Roy closed his mouth and, with a slight smile, nodded.

"OK, I don't suppose they do Murden's pop anymore.
I'll have whatever you're having."

As I was walking to the kitchen I noticed a small drop
of blood on the back of the hand clutching the knife. It was

odd because I could feel no pain of injury. I examined the skin of both hands but there was no apparent lesion. I threw the knife into the cluttered sink and rinsed the blood under the tap.

I opened the fridge.

Since Tina's departure the fridge had almost been emptied, but now it was completely packed with bottles of Murden's pop, with all the varieties of flavour. I bent over and selected a Cherryade and an Orangeade. I removed the tops with a bottle opener and thrust two drinking straws into each bottle.

I carried them back into the room.

It was then that I made a startling discovery about Roy.

I placed the Orangeade next to him and noticed that he was sitting in a rather uncomfortable position with his head inclined backwards at an unusual angle. I then did what I'd never done before. I gave him an investigative prod. When we were children we must have touched when we played or fought, but never an investigative prod.

Roy immediately slumped on to the floor.

I tried to turn him over and sit him up, but found that red lentils, mixed with a small quantity of black-eyed beans, were pouring from a tear in his throat. The more that I tried to manoeuvre him, the more the tear gaped opened and issued the lentils. Even a slight compression caused a torrent of pulses to cascade across the carpet.

The simplest was to lay him on his back and not touch him.

I tried to make sense of the whole thing. All this time Roy was nothing more than a sack full of legumes. The implications were profound. Our whole childhood together assumed a new interpretation. The prospects of my wife fancying Roy became absurd. Even his contribution to her study on the connection between orthodontic correction and male sexual perversion instantly lost plausibility.

I must admit I felt some relief. My self-esteem rose. I was a miserable failure in life, yet more than a sack of legumes.

But my problems remained. For the thousandth time I dabbed my tongue along the inside of my mouth. Throughout the emptiness of the day the false teeth were constantly in and out of my mouth as I indulged in oral self-examination. I came to no conclusions but, by the end, my mouth was starting to feel sore. I really could have done with Roy's advice.

There seemed to be little further point in trying to communicate with Roy. I sat down on the chair that Roy had been sitting in and I sucked hard on the straw of my cherryade until it made a heavy draining sound. I then picked up Roy's orangeade and drank that as well. With some satisfaction I put my feet on the sack of lentils and belched loudly.

The next morning there seemed little else to do but dispose of the sack of lentils that had once comprised Roy's mistaken entity. I collected several black bags together and using one bag to reinforce another I gradually sealed up the troublesome bulk with strong sticky tape.

The whole thing took much longer than I had anticipated. Not only the wrapping, but the lentils had scattered over most of the carpet and even into the hall. Tediously I brushed them into a dustpan and added them to the greater mass.

I hadn't slept at all well, my gums had been aching all night and then having to sweep Roy up totally exhausted me. I now had to face carrying him out to the car and driving him to the rubbish tip.

I managed to roll the parcel through the hall, through the kitchen and force it through the back door. In full view of the neighbours, the postman, the milkman, the children in the school playground, the road sweeper and, making one of his rare appearances, the window cleaner, I compressed Roy into the boot of the car.

We drove up the street followed by the rich exhaust of a badly tuned engine.

We entered the rubbish tip by driving over a ramp past a deserted checkpoint. I paused for a minute. My mouth seemed very sore. I made a toothless grin into the driving mirror and I suddenly realised that I wasn't wearing the false teeth. I thought back to getting up in the morning. I had a distinct image of the glass being empty. In my haste to rise and sweep up the lentils I think I assumed, without any checking, that I'd forgotten to take the teeth out the night before. Suddenly I felt naked in a public place and immediately hid my mouth behind my hand.

I drove up to the balustrade that overlooked the skips for dumping the rubbish. I opened the boot and managed to get the parcel onto the road. I now faced the task of lifting it over the balustrade and cursed myself for not dividing the rather formidable quantity of lentils into two or more loads. I managed to raise the parcel high enough to use the balustrade as a fulcrum and then dropped the whole thing over the edge into the skip below.

The skip was three-quarters empty and the parcel hit the bottom with an impressive resonance. So well was it taped up that, despite the fall, it remained intact apart from a tiny rupture. I could see a small pile of lentils forming like sand from an hourglass. To the right of my parcel was an almost identical black, taped parcel, partly submerged in the refuse. It had obviously been dumped a day or two earlier. Instead of leaking lentils it was leaking rice. The parcels looked like two ominous, black eggs waiting to disgorge sinister surprises at the end of their periods of incubation. It was as if a bird of dereliction was laying its eggs here in the rubbish tip.

Near to where the rice merged with the lentils there was a wooden box that seemed familiar.

Despite there being a notice to the public, warning them that, should they remove anything from the dump, they faced the threat of prosecution, I climbed over the balustrade and lowered myself down into the skip. I crouched down by the wooden box and opened it.

Inside there was a battalion of plastic soldiers. What was particularly odd about them was that they were my soldiers. It was my own toy box from childhood. It occurred to me that in an era of non-perishable artefacts, our toys will be with us indefinitely. Maybe dispersed and irretrievable, but none the less they are all out there somewhere, buried in rubbish tips.

I quickly snatched the box up and climbed out of the skip. At this point I think I must have been seen. I could hear distant voices and two figures started to run toward me. With the box under my arm I managed to swing over the balustrade. I climbed into my car and drove away.

The box was beside me on the passenger seat, once again I opened it. As I examined the contents I could see that they were exactly the same toy soldiers that I had as a small boy. I studied them carefully, picking each one up at a time. I recognised their individual blemishes, even the battle scars from their distant wars.

Suddenly I wanted to share my find. It was just too remarkable a coincidence. I suppose ideally I should have shared it with Roy, who would have known the soldiers as well as I did. Unfortunately recent events had revealed him to be nothing more than lentils. Then I thought of my son. I could share my find with Thomas. Show him what toys were like in my time.

I glanced at my watch. Thomas would be walking home from school by now. Thomas was a bit of a sore point. When Tina was preparing to go away for her course, it was decided that I was too useless to cater for him. It was decided that my parents in law should look after him, his father being such an incompetent.

With Tina's recent moral growth spurt, against my own natural tendencies, we'd become vegetarian. To be quite honest, I was completely sick of hearing the problems of deriving whole protein from vegetable sources. Needless to say, Tina, with her rapidly expanding intellect quickly grasped the solution. Personally I was struggling a bit. I had it drilled into me that the eight essential amino acids are

> Isoleucine
>
> Leucine
>
> Lycine
>
> Methionine
>
> Phenylalanine
>
> Threonine
>
> Tryptophan
>
> Valine

Any one particular source of vegetable protein does not contain all the essential amino acids and hence must be eaten in conjunction with other vegetable sources to ensure the vital mix is achieved.

Nuts must be eaten with beans. Beans must be eaten with grains. Grains must be eaten with dairy products. To be quite honest my simple comprehension gave out and since Tina was determined to make Thomas entirely out of vegetable matter I forfeited the right to look after my son in my wife's absence.

Just before she left, Tina softened the blow by claiming that, since her parents lived at walking distance from Thomas's school, that it would save me time in having to take him to and from school. Save me time? My incompetence is so profound that I have all the time in the world.

As I was cruising along I suppose I shouldn't have had the soldiers out on the passenger seat. I suppose I shouldn't have divided them into two factions and let them declare war on one another. If I hadn't been guiding the individual soldiers through their battle plans I might have actually seen what happened on the road.

There was a soft bump and the left wheel of the car went over something. Quickly I stopped.

When I got out to see what had happened, I found a small dead monkey lying behind the car. It had no injury apart from a trickle of blood from one nostril. The monkey looked bedraggled and pathetic. I could find no explanation as to what had happened.

Leaving the car at an angle, half on the road half on the pavement, driver's door wide open, the engine still running and the toy soldiers scattered on the floor of the car, I simply walked away.

My mouth was sore and the cold air exacerbated it. I covered my mouth with my hand and made the rest of my journey home on foot.

I unlocked the front door and the first thing that I noticed was that the light was winking on the answer phone. I thought that it might be Tina at last. I pressed the button. It wasn't Tina, it was her mother.

'…we're a bit worried. We haven't heard from Tina since we assumed she'd left for the conference. We were just wondering if you knew what was happening. We rang the conference centre but they say that she didn't arrive. They apparently rang your number but they said that they repeatedly got through to a moron babbling nonsense about false teeth. Reg said that it certainly sounded like you, I must admit I tend to agree. I must go now, Thomas is due back from school. Can you give me a ring and let me know what is happening.'

The close of the message was punctuated with a beep. I felt a surge of guilt. As soon as I located my false teeth I would go straight round and visit my parents-in-law and apologise for being such a lousy, indolent husband to their beloved and long suffering daughter. I closed my eyes and saw two drowned whales decomposing on a deserted beach.

I had to find the missing false teeth. They weren't in the glass on my bedside table. I pulled open all the drawers and emptied them on the floor. I ransacked the wardrobe, ripping Tina's dresses from the hangers.

I looked under Tina's bed. There was a thin scattering of rice.

For the first time I fully appreciated the complement of amino acids. Rice and lentils. The construction of whole protein and the desire for sustenance.

I ran downstairs and ripped out the fuse box. Upturned the refrigerator. Smashed the bureau with an axe. I still couldn't find the false teeth.

The phone rang. I went into the hall and started ripping at the wires. Suddenly I heard a voice talking to me in a slow, deliberate tone.

I pressed my hands to my ears. The voice vanished. I took my hands away and it came back. The growing darkness of the early evening made the whole situation eerie.

I then noticed somebody was watching me through the letter box.

The voice spoke again, calmly asking me to open the door.

No. Of course not. Not now. I'm much too busy. I must sort out the matter of the teeth.

Several sharp objects within my mouth touched my tongue.

I rushed upstairs to the bathroom and flicked the light switch on to look in the mirror. Nothing happened. There was no electricity.

Downstairs, I could hear the splintering of wood as the rude man I'd seen peering through the letter box began to smash the front door down.

In the gloom I peered at my open mouth in the mirror. Fortunately a periodic blue light flashed through the window. In the brief instants of illumination I could clearly see, embedded in the gum, two rows of tiny, growing teeth.

I felt a sense of relief. The curious ordeal was over. I experienced a strong feeling of optimism. Wait till I tell Tina and Thomas. I could even see limited hope for Roy. This was certainly a positive sign that the recent disruptions to our lives were over and my wife's breasts would finally return to their former state of adolescent perfection.

The Nettle Eaters

1. Pip, Beatrice and Timmy

I always thought when Pip died he would go the way of Timmy the crab. But I was mistaken.

Unlike Pip, Timmy the crab lived his life along the stretch of shoreline where we were occasional visitors. Timmy revealed himself, not to us but to the family next to us. He was christened by the father and was in excellent form.

'Timmy run Timmy jump Timmy stop Timmy through the hoop Timmy start Timmy hop Timmy pinch Timmy whoops Timmy oops Timmy Timmy Timmy Timmy …'

Timmy snapped his claws and moved with splendid energy. I watched with jealousy over the shoulders of the happy gathering of children. This extraordinary family could fashion intimate relationships that bridged the species.

Pip seemed oblivious. But I suspected the colourful deck chair that provided his comfort disguised his opinion of the circus that performed a few yards in front of him.

'Can we find a crab like Timmy?'

No answer.

'Please.'

Nothing.

Pip was a man of few words. What he was doing, I had no idea. He was just sitting. No paper, book, bag of sweets, ice cream. He seemed just to be thinking. A handkerchief tied at the corners on his head.

The circus dispersed in the rising heat and I forgot about Timmy. Time slid the ocean backward and then forward again across the sand and we prepared to leave.

I noticed the family had gone and I searched their area of occupation for Timmy in the hope that I might squeeze a little more entertainment from the diminutive crab. Eventually I found him lying dead by a tributary next to a rock.

He pinched and wiggled no more. Nor was he lying nobly in state waiting for the water to carry him homeward one last time. He was one third buried in the sand, protruding at an ungainly angle of approximately thirty degrees.

I imagined Pip's fate would be similar from his sexual labours with Beatrice. He would be found days later hanging out of the torn bedding at an angle of thirty degrees with arms stiff in an empty embrace.

But I was wrong. Pip's death was a carefully orchestrated, brutal murder.

Is it not the case that prior to such a horrific murder, strange and inexplicable events occur? Only when the full crime is finally solved can sense be made of these peculiar details that form its constitution.

For instance I suddenly noticed that I hadn't got a belly button.

Maybe I never had one. That dimple that revealed more than the presence of a mother that I had never formally known. It expressed belonging. Definitely the space between the trouser and the vest was empty. The principle of the umbilical cord was suddenly placed in doubt and I became isolated from my fellow mammals.

This changed everything. I needed to know if my brother was the same but the question didn't go down well. He was going through a particularly pernicious puberty that denied him the means for rational response. I had to physically take control of the situation and grabbed at his shirt. He responded by falling on to me and we ended up rolling across the floor. I was desperate.

'Tell me. I need to know.'

'Piss off you little pervert.'

His voice squeaked and oscillated in the ill-defined register between boy and man. The changes were making him really strange and I began to distrust him.

A growth spurt had suddenly rendered him both bigger and stronger so naturally he ended up on top. He made the mistake of assuming that he had won and that I had submitted. He stood up and foolishly turned his back to me. I shot up and pushed him forward as hard as I could. The top of his head went through the window and jammed into a perfectly round, bloody hole in the glass.

'Get me out you little shit.'

I missed an opportunity. When he was trapped in the glass I could have easily slipped round, pulled up the shirt and identified the situation of his belly button. However, we temporally became unified in the panic of crisis.

I pulled at him and he staggered backward onto the bed, one hand was over his eye.

'Something's in it. Get it out. Get it out.'

I pulled his hand away and held open the eye between thumb and forefinger. The upper and lower lids fought my grip and twitched with an indefatigable electricity. I could see a limpet of glass clinging to the pupil of my brother's left eye.

'Are you blind? Can you see?

'Of course I can. Just get it out you little wanker.'

The white was crossed with raging red veins but the delicate black circle of the pupil appeared to remain unharmed beneath the splinter of glass. The fragment was the shape of Timmy the crab. I watched the salty tide rise in what looked like a miniature ocean. The waves rose and beat at the feet of the crab but failed to displace it. I would have to do it myself. I first considered levering it with my thumbnail encrusted with grime and simply flick the shard off. This solution was undeniably crude and carried some risk.

Instead I ran to Beatrice's bedside cabinet and removed her pair of excellent forceps. When I got back, I noticed the tide had flooded now in both my brother's eyes. The right eye had come out in sympathy. I pressed the lid almost up to the eyebrow with my thumb and prepared to dive in with the forceps. The eyeball looked shocked and tried to squirm in its confinement.

I had to act quickly. Not just to minimalize my brother's suffering but the shouting and sudden activity had disturbed Beatrice's afternoon nap. I could hear a slow, heavy arthritic footstep on the stair.

This was no easy matter. I managed to get one of Timmy's legs in the grasp of the forceps. I tried to flick it but nothing happened. I hadn't reckoned with the cohesive effect of my brother's sissy tears. I flicked it harder. Then harder still.

The footsteps were closing in. The door handle was beginning to move.

Suddenly to my relief the glass pinged away into a corner of the room. Unfortunately, stuck to the glass was a substantial part of the cornea. It left a neat black hole.

I tried to underplay the situation.

'I think it's OK now.'

For a second I actually thought it was OK. Then the clear jelly of the aqueous humour began to ooze from the hole, followed by the lens still attached to the suspensory ligament. There was a brief pause, then the whole thing flooded with blood. This was a complete revelation for me. I had believed in good faith that the eyes are the windows of the incorporeal mind. Surely, the blood vessels went no deeper than the sclera. Beyond that, one encountered the start of the phosphorescent globe of the geist. Where all the viscera were coming from, I had no idea. My brother was as astonished as I was.

Our screams merged and the door opened to provide an aperture sufficient to deliver the formidable Beatrice to the proceedings.

I didn't wait around. In a well-practised manner I opened the window, slid down the sloping roof, scrambled down the drainpipe and leapt onto the lawn cushioned with moss. I ran off up the path and disappeared from view.

The disappearance of the belly button wasn't the only strange occurrence. There was much more to come.

When I reached the lane at the bottom of the garden, without pausing, I climbed the steep railway embankment. With a careful eye for steam engines, I crossed the lines and went down the other side to the wasteland. I tripped over a root and found myself rolling over and over, narrowly missing a pernicious clump of stinging nettles at the bottom. The world became a cylinder spinning around me. What I couldn't understand was why the very house that I had sought to escape from was now orbiting my head. I came to a stop at the bottom.

I closed my eyes and lay on the ground waiting for the dizziness to pass. When I opened them again the house was still there. Clearly it wasn't Pip and Beatrice's. It had the same appearance but was considerably smaller.

Unsteadily I walked round it. I suspected that all of the dimensions of Pip and Beatrice's house had been exactly halved. All the features were exactly the same, the colour of the paint, the windows, the red tiled roof. I tried looking through the windows but it was too dark to see inside. I carefully opened the front door and peered into the hall but I still couldn't see anything. I stooped down and squeezed through the door. The hall had the same pattern of carpet and furniture as Beatrice and Pip's house. My shoulders jammed in the front door and I bumped my head on the hall ceiling. I eased myself through and on all fours crept to the back of the house. I started to push the kitchen door open with my forefinger and I caught a glimpse of the periphery of a moving frock. I thought I heard a voice whisper to the effect the boy was coming.

Quickly I scrambled out of the tiny house, back up the bank and off in the other direction.

I knew I couldn't go back home and would have to stay away forever.

My plan appeared sound and worked well for a while but I hadn't taken account of the appetite. I just became too hungry. Finally, as the sun was setting, I was propelled home against my better judgement.

The front door was unlocked and I crept into the hall. Strangely, it was as if nothing had happened. Dinner was being served and I was called to my place.

Stringy meat with gristle, bone and eyeballs was served from the black pot in the middle of the table and we all got on with the sordid task of ingestion and digestion.

Beatrice and Pip didn't mention the unfortunate events of the afternoon. It was all a bit silent. But then meals usually consisted of few words.

My brother seemed subdued. He had a sinister black patch over his left eye, which barely concealed a bulky dressing. When I sat down next to him I noticed that there were tiny stitches along the cut in his head. The hair at both sides of the cut had been shaved as if the top of his head had been completely severed and then neatly sewn back on.

I wondered whether to pretend nothing had happened and make a surprised enquiry as to how my brother had befallen this accident.

I thought better of it.

I assumed after the meal, I would be flogged or something. Not that I'd ever been flogged before but my misdeed seemed quite extensive.

After the meal we were sent straight to bed leaving Beatrice and Pip to their rituals and routines. There was no mention of my brother's eye whatsoever. Looking back it could have been that Beatrice and Pip had noticed the occurrence of unusual events as well as me. Possibly they had some sense of impending death. Maybe my misdemeanour was mild in comparison to these weightier matters.

My brother and I lay quietly in our separate beds.

I felt a bit inhibited to mention the eye but managed a sort of apology.

'I'm sorry about earlier on.'

'That's all right. Binocular. Monocular. What the hell.'

I still wanted to know if he had a belly button but I didn't want to start the fight up again. He seemed different anyway. As if now bearing a stigmata had caused him to reflect.

'How long do you think we've been children now? Is it the handful of years that Pip and Beatrice suggest is normal of the mammalians? Or is it more like the thirty odd years that I've notched on the bedpost with my penknife?' He casually pointed to his system of measure.

'Who are Pip and Beatrice? Are they father and mother, uncle and aunt, grandfather and grandmother? Who are they? We've never been told. If you ask me, something odd is going on.'

I took this to be an oblique reference to the belly button crisis. I guessed he was indicating there was an anomaly concerning our births and the whole of our childhoods. It seemed we were both alienated from a normal mammalian origin. But at least the mutual feeling of alienation seemed to be bringing us together. For the first time the distance between us lessened.

Despite my brother losing his eye, the world seemed to have slightly improved.

The cool summer breeze entered the room through the hole in the window that we'd created that afternoon. With it carried the dreamy sound of a dog barking far off, somewhere beyond the embankment. I began to feel relaxed and sleepy. The darkening blue sky seemed to be magnified in transmission through the clear portal. Gradually it filled with summer stars.

There were questions for Pip and Beatrice. I thought these could wait till the morning.

I was mistaken.

The next morning we learned that Beatrice was dead.

2. Natural and Unnatural Causes

My brother and I came downstairs for breakfast. Beatrice would have set the breakfast things the night before but it was immediately noticeable that the toast rack was devoid of toast and the cereal bowls empty of cereal. Given

Beatrice's strict habits, what could have been a surer sign of her death?

Pip was sitting at the table with his hands to his face, weeping copiously. Dr A was upstairs tending to Beatrice's body.

Pip composed himself.

'I'm afraid I have bad news for you, boys. Beatrice is dead. She has given up the geist. Late last night after our sexual toils had been completed, after what had been a difficult day, Beatrice suddenly realised her heart was slowing down. Shortly after two a.m. it stopped altogether. This was not a good omen, boys. But I question if the failing body is prepared to give up so quickly on the geist and eject it to oblivion. On the other hand, I cannot believe the geist would give up on the body on the meagre ground that the heart was stopping. Surely for anyone living a life with the energy and vitality of Beatrice, it would imply that a powerful momentum has built up that guarantees life will carry on for some time after the natural function of the bodily organs has ceased. Just as a cricket ball continues to live a life of momentum after leaving the bowler's hand. This may extend for hours, days, possibly even a modest number of years. Maybe indefinitely. Yes, she was frightened, boys. We both were. We held hands. We talked of our first meeting. Our first kiss. Our first spring. Our first glimpse of damselfly, meteorite and hoar frost. We filled the space with words, hoping that it would never end. Then it happened, boys. Just before the dawn, the air issued finally from her lungs like a wind bursting from inflated bellows in which the leather has become inflexible and spent. I tried to capture the last breath in my hands, boys. With a cry of grief I tried to stop it escaping and return it to its rightful place. But it moved in all directions too quickly and I lost control. My hands snatched emptily in the air as the breath divided into an infinity of microscopic particles. Beatrice lay where she fell, crumpled and empty.'

We tried to console Pip but I suppose we were uncertain about our own feelings.

My brother and I formed a solemn procession behind Pip. We climbed the stairs to witness the remnant of Beatrice. We entered the darkened room. Beatrice was still lying where she had fallen. Dr A appeared to be toiling with balms in the hope of achieving at least some degree of resurrection. It was obvious, I think, to all of us that it was hopeless.

Certainly Dr A was shaking his head. He packed up his bag and started to leave.

'There is really nothing more I can do. Do not be alarmed if there are post mortem movements. They are known as 'Sommer's movements'. Do not take significance in them. They are due to the onset of rigor mortis and in no way do they imply that Beatrice is coming back to life. My advice is to place her in the safe hands of an undertaker. They are practiced in the care of the deceased.'

Typically Pip declined. He preferred to manage on his own.

He insisted on a vigil. My brother and I agreed to accompany him. We left him only as he made preparations of the body.

'Do you want us to help you lift her onto the bed?'

For whatever reasons, Pip decided to leave her where she was. When we returned, Beatrice was still in the same position on the floor but was covered with a large embroidered sheet. Four candles marked the corners of the rectangle in which she lay.

The day was long and depressing and none of us spoke or ate. As evening drew on we noticed a twitching under the sheet. At first it was just a movement of fingers but eventually it was the entire body.

Suddenly Beatrice sat up and threw the sheet off as if making ready for escape.

We lacked resources to help us cope with the situation.

The three of us lifted the heavy sideboard from the corner of the room and placed it over her to contain her. It continued to bump and scrape on the floor. As fast as we could we gathered heavy objects to weigh it down.

Sometimes she giggled like a little girl and then it would unexpectedly turn into a deep, guttural, mocking laughter. The conversation she had on her first meeting with Pip reiterated in her larynx but was twisted into a vulgar vomiting. She mimicked their first kiss and then transformed it into a prolonged farting noise. She negated their first summer. She swatted the damselfly. Spat on the meteor. Pissed on the hoar-frost.

'She's coming back boys. See, she's coming back.'

We shouted against the hubbub.

'No, Pip. Dr A said we were not to think that. Please come downstairs with us.'

We tried to grab his arms but he pushed us away.

'My sweetheart. My sweetheart.'

'No, Pip. It isn't Beatrice anymore. She's dead. You must realise that. Come downstairs.'

Despite the ballast, the sideboard tipped forward and crashed to the floor, knocking over the candles. Three went out but the forth set the curtains alight.

We managed to pull them down and started to stamp the flames out.

As we were doing this, Pip bent over the writhing body with arms outstretched to hold her down. Beatrice grabbed him by the throat with both hands.

Luckily, we had beaten the flames out. We rushed to Pip and tried to release him from Beatrice's grasp. We struggled as he turned purple and emitted sounds of strangulation. As I tried to pull Beatrice back, my brother managed to unlock her hands from Pip's throat.

Just as my brother had done that, Beatrice's hand escaped from his grasp and with astonishing rapidity reached under the bed. There was an owl screech and the chamber pot came crashing down on Pip's head. Pip fell unconscious and stale urine sloshed all over us. Between us we managed to drag Pip from the room.

Before she could follow I slammed the door and held it tight. She fought to open it. My brother acquired tools and nailed the door safely shut.

We took Pip downstairs and gave him sweet tea infused with whiskey. As he drank the tea we placed a generous bandage resembling a turban on his wounded brow.

Eventually the screams above subsided to a murmur. By dawn it had virtually stopped.

Pip sat in his chair, beaten and defeated.

'Boys, I have been a fool. We must bury the dead even if it is only to prevent them from venting spleen on the living.'

Five days later we had the funeral.

Mourners gathered at the side of the newly dug grave.

It was a clear sunny day and a host of insects attended the diversity of flowers. In connection to the accumulation of strange occurrences I noticed the presence of policemen, as if they were gathering at a potential crime site. Scores of plain clothed policemen with the trademark disguise of mackintosh, bowler hat and fake walrus moustache loitered in the bushes. They spoke surreptitiously into hidden walkie-talkies creating the effect they were secretly conversing with the pollinators on the summer blooms. I should have known that a horrendous assault was about to be committed.

Beatrice was swallowed by the stony subsoil along with a few choruses of 'Abide with Me'. Then the attendants of the funeral pushed off in different directions. The mourners came back to our house. The policemen that had infiltrated the mourners slipped back into the shadows of street corners and underpasses.

Back home, we provided the mourners with the traditional funereal fare of salmon paste sandwiches and tea in large pots that had been brewed for far too long.

Eventually the mourners sympathetically departed and left us to reformulate our lives in the absence of Beatrice.

It was shortly after this that my brother and I realised that Pip had been horribly murdered.

Pip went upstairs to relieve a full bladder from the stewed tea and my brother and I sat down on the settee to compose ourselves. It was his first piss as a fully qualified widower.

With the death and burial done, it felt as if a burden had been lifted. The pair of us dozed where we sat. In my pleasant half-conscious state I listened to the singing of skylarks above the roof of the house and the distant buzzing of the pollinators. I had pleasant, flickering fragments of dreams that occur sometimes when I'm just about to fall asleep. I saw Pip in the distance, waving frantically at me through the window.

I immediately woke up and realised Pip was absent. A whole hour had passed since he'd gone up stairs. This was too long for the purpose of a piss. I rose to my feet. My sudden movement woke my brother. We called up to Pip but there was no reply.

We crept up the stairs and searched each room starting with his own. But it was in our own bedroom that we found him. The crime was so savage and complete that any remnant of skin or bone had completely dispersed. All that was left of the old man was a portrait in oils lying beside the open window. Its gilded frame was peeling and the varnish, darkened with age, was cracked.

Despite the damage, the portrait was noble and undoubtedly depicted Pip as we would have liked to remember him.

3. Bosch and Callot

Needless to say we were shocked. We were not sure what had happened. We were not even sure anything had happened. Neither of us had seen the picture of Pip before.

There was a sort of silence that lasted for a couple of minutes.

Then sirens screamed and blue stroboscopes attacked our senses. Through the window we could see a 'scene of crime' cordon had been placed round the house. Armed police officers with guns and helmets with darkened visors poured out of a van and scattered with pre-established harmony. The front door splintered and DI Bosch and Sergeant Callot rose majestically up the stairway on the steely armature of a police gantry.

I appreciated the extent of the operation. Almost hidden in the background I made out a myriad of smaller uniformed policemen who had failed to grow to the statutory height. They were furiously operating levers and ratchet wheels that controlled the police gantry.

The gantry came to a halt a few feet from our bedroom door.

ID flicked open in Bosch's hand and shut within a nanosecond.

He switched on a megaphone.

> I must warn you in advance that ID can only be validated by reference to further documentation which, in turn, can only be validated by further documentation. Some claim this process leads to an infinite regress and cannot establish identification with anything even approaching certainty. I say bollocks. Let's truncate this logistic series before it gets out of hand and just get on with the matter in hand.
>
> (A snigger erupted from one of the policemen operating the gantry)
>
> So, what's been going on here? What little misdemeanour has catapulted your lives into the stark theatre of the crime scene? What are the facts? The little old man you refer to as 'Pip', who coincidentally bears an indeterminate relationship to you, goes missing

following the funeral of his beloved wife. Dramatically it accelerates into a murder enquiry. It turns out to be one of those strange cases where there's no body, no motive, no suspect. That is until now. I have good reason to believe, from extensive training and long experience of police methods, that the identity of both the suspect and crime are beginning to merge together.

(Another snigger erupted from behind the gantry)

DI Bosch's eyes pinned on my brother.

So, you really have no idea of the whereabouts of this indeterminate relation. Would you object if I searched your person, Sir?

Bosch nodded minimally to Callot. Callott stepped off the gantry and stood before my brother.

He tore off my brother's bandage. The remnant of eye gaped like a dried-up fish's eye. However, there must have been some remnant of freshness because the eye oozed a small quantity of clear liquid that trickled down my brother's cheek.

My brother let out a snort of contempt and turned his head to the side. Callott pulled him up by the lapels and turned to Bosch as if for further instruction. Bosch still addressed my brother through the megaphone. His voice still bore the superficial politeness of the consummate policemen that barely disguises contempt and disgust.

I know what you are thinking, Sir. You are thinking, 'this policeman is so, so stupid that he believes there's something hidden behind the bandage.' No Sir, I know perfectly well that I will not find a corpse in the vacated orbit of your eye. Or even that I expect that Pip will actually leap out of the eye socket with even more health and vigour than he's had for years. If you think that you have nothing hidden behind the bandage, I'm afraid you are mistaken, Sir. You see, I don't even need to peer into your damaged eye to know that although the lens and ciliary muscles have been dislodged, the retina is largely intact. I know this from the medical notes from the hospital where your eye was treated a few days ago. We can take you down to Police Headquarters and peel away the retina from the back of your eye without any need to recourse to anaesthetic. Police methods have moved on since the era of the bicycle clip and the bobby on the beat. We can process your retina like a film from a camera. We can derive actual footage of your murderous assault on the victim. We can strip out your eardrum and reproduce the cries of agony as Pip fell under your vicious attack. We can even drill down into the sensitive saliva glands surrounding your tongue and hear for ourselves the motive for your crime.

Callot let go of my brother. He slumped to the floor miserable and humiliated. The place filled up with uniformed officers with truncheons. They dragged him back on to his feet and constrained both of us. Bosch switched off the megaphone. He leaned forward on the gantry and pinched my brother roughly on the cheek.

'Don't take it too badly. It's all for the good of humanity. Violent crimes of this nature have increased dramatically. But have no fears. The population of policemen is expanding automatically to counteract it. To every new criminal born, two policemen are born. It's the balance of nature. If the population of naughty little bunny rabbits increases because they're eating the good farmer's seeds, then the population of buzzards also increases to gobble up the bunny rabbits. We're just the servants of the people. To demonstrate in a clear and unambiguous way that Sergeant Callot and I are nothing other than lovable human beings and bear no personal malice to you, we will dance a merry, comical dance just for you.'

Callot stepped back onto the gantry next to Bosch.

They adjusted their braces until their trousers were drawn tightly into their groins and the cracks of their arses. As the gantry was slowly lowered frantic music started up and both policemen performed a fast and intricate jig in perfect unison. I found it horrifically compelling and realised my foot was tapping in time. Then suddenly I experienced the pure horror of the situation. I wondered if Bosch had been telling the truth. If the policemen were reproducing, how was this possible? I could see clearly from the stricture of their trousers that neither policeman had balls.

4. The Police Headquarters

My brother and I were divided between two police cars. I travelled with Sergeant Callot and my brother with DI Bosch.

To maintain the air of friendly intent, Sergeant Callot offered me a sweetie from a white paper bag that he drew from his pocket. I accepted but instead of allowing me to peek inside the bag and make my own choice, he rapidly plucked out a large, black lozenge between his thumb and forefinger. He dangled it over my head. I turned my face upwards and let my mouth gape open so my quivering tongue could surge forward to greet the glistening morsel. To my surprise he slapped it on the middle of my forehead leaving my tongue disappointed and redundant. Gradually the feeling of disappointment assuaged. Despite the policeman's unconventional approach to confectionery, it felt as if the sweetie was melting in my mouth and filling it with sweet liqueurs.

I was taken through the concrete corridors of the police headquarters and introduced to Dr Baker who was to take a statement from me. I must admit it was all turning out to be quite jolly.

I expressed concern about what might happen to my brother. Dr Baker winked and opened the door behind me. I could hear continuous waves of my brother's laugher echoing throughout the building.

'You mustn't worry. Naturally we are disturbed at his recent violent behaviour that has resulted in what we term 'a walking corpse'. In keeping with our policy of moral agency we have withdrawn a prescribed amount of goodwill. But this is by no means absolute. We haven't been quite as nice to him as we have to you. Nor have we been at all nasty. For instance, unlike you, he hasn't been offered a sweetie. However that is not the end of the matter. If he cooperates with our questioning it is highly likely that he will be offered one at a later time. As you can hear, he is suffering no distress. In fact he seems to be rather enjoying himself. It is a common misapprehension that police interrogation is a nasty brutal affair. This is untrue, it is often stimulating and rewarding.'

I must admit I began to feel quite a lot of relief. For the first time for quite a long while I felt positively happy. In fact I felt very, very happy.

I splurged everything that had happened to my brother and me to Dr Baker in reverse order. It went from Pip's disappearance all the way back to the all too brief life of Timmy the crab. Dr Baker was professional and calm. From time to time he injected a question.

'So when Pip effectively refused to find an equivalent of Timmy to entertain you on the beach that day, did you experience resentment?'

On happy occasions such as this, I have the bad habit of rocking backward and forward on my chair. Another wave of laugher echoed from my brother's interrogation. I found myself laughing in unison. The joy turned into an uncontrollable ecstasy and I tumbled over backwards on the chair. I then performed a further backward somersault and ended flat on my face.

I picked up my head and before me on the floor was the lozenge that Sergeant Callot had stuck on my forehead.

Now it seemed less like a sweetie and more like a squashed, segmented worm. Where it had been placed my on forehead, I could feel a raw Y-shaped groove in the skin. Threads of anaesthetic saliva still connected the groove to the leech. As we parted company the threads became increasingly stretched until finally they snapped. My brother's laughter instantly turned to screams of torture. My ecstatic joy turned into a throbbing headache. Dr Baker's torso changed into thorax, prothorax, mesothorax and metathorax. He turned out not to be sitting in a chair but dangling threateningly from the ceiling with antennae twitching. His mandible snapped open and shut issuing an incomprehensible signal. The forewing and hind wing started to open as if he was about to take flight.

I decided I'd had enough and legged it.

I fled into the corridor. The hard concrete interior of the police headquarters had somehow been replaced by a maze of cells and tunnels. I hadn't the faintest idea where I was. The walls glowed an eerie white. I ran and ran but had no way of assessing my progress in the repeating structure. Somewhere behind me I heard a dry rustling as a million wings started up.

I had to get out of here. Then the answer came to me. I realised I was running on what gave the impression of stretched parchment. I stopped and examined the floor. It was glowing white not because of soft internal lighting but because daylight was showing through. The entire police headquarters was made of nothing more than layers of paper. Frantically I started to tear at it. Layers came away in my hands. The structure became too weak to support my weight. There was a tearing sound and suddenly I found myself spinning through the air. I landed arse-down in a gigantic cow pat.

Above me the police headquarters was dangling from a magnificent oak tree.

I didn't stop for long. I had no idea where I was. I continued running along lanes, rough tracks and bridle paths. I ran through valleys, woodland and glades until I reached the familiarity of the outskirts of the town. I then made my way back to Pip's house.

The first thing I saw was a police car cruising up and down the road in front of Pip's house. I assumed they were looking for me so I eased myself unnoticed though the passageway to the back garden and climbed over the embankment. Once again I tripped over a root and found myself rolling over and over towards the little house behind Pip's. The first time I came here I managed to avoid the clump of stinging nettles. This time I ploughed straight through the middle of it. My short trousers and tee-shirt allowed me little protection. My arms and legs came up in those little hard white lumps that accompany nettle stings. I lay in agony but I couldn't stop. I picked myself up and ran straight into the little house. I thrust myself through the front door and squeezed through the hall into the kitchen.

To my surprise Pip was sitting, compressed into the corner. Both of us virtually filled the space. The thing is that it wasn't really Pip. In all ways he looked like Pip. He was wearing the same clothes. He had the same face. However, it wasn't Pip, it was Mr Peacock. It was just that Mr Peacock happened to look remarkably similar to Pip. I found this totally confusing. My encounter with Mr Peacock was hopelessly muddled and contradictory. I know it is not satisfactory but the clearest way I can describe what happened next is by dividing up the events as far as I can remember them and placing them in two separate columns.

5. Mr Peacock

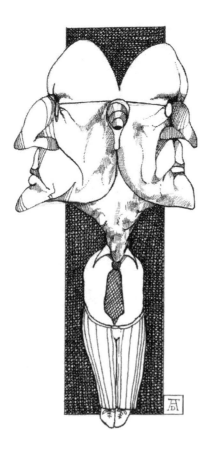

'My dear, dear boy, how are you? You've been through a rough time but you are always welcome to take refuge here. I know that you are hiding from the police but I assure you that you are perfectly safe here. In fact, if your brother ever gets

'My dear, dear boy. How are you? You must feel very confused. There is much that I have to explain. I think you are well aware that in any murder enquiry nothing is as it seems. Reality has been pulled from under our feet.

out of police custody, he is welcome too.

'Come don't be shy. The space is a little restricted. It is a consequence of capitation restrictions. I'm afraid they are strictly necessary for the department to remain solvent.

'Squeeze up close to me. Isn't this cosy. We are sharing the same space and air. I can feel the warmth generating from your virile body like a three kilowatt electric fire.

'But look. Your arms and legs are covered with nettle stings.'

He gently parted my hair and seemed genuinely grieved.

'Even your delicate brow has not escaped those cruel, cruel nettles. Come, let me soothe your stings with fresh dockings.'

Mr Peacock slid open one of the drawers in the dresser. It was packed with neatly cut rows of dock leaves.

Mr Peacock winked at me.

'Freshly picked this morning in anticipation of a crisis such as this.'

He carefully selected a particularly succulent leaf and crushed it in his fist.

'See how the embrocation seeps from the stem. It always reminds me of the consistency of semen.'

'You must be thinking what is this place? Where am I? Is this queer old man going to take an unhealthy interest in my nettle rash? That is most certainly not the case.

'In a nutshell you are in the temporary accommodation of the 'Independent Police Complaints Commission'.

"I think probably you have already guessed something odd has been happening for some time. We believe that it is the police themselves that are at fault in this enquiry. To adopt the appropriate technical term: it is most definitely an 'inside job'.

'I must explain our procedure. In recent times public faith in the modern policemen has diminished. When a crime scene is about to materialise, the IPCC automatically forms an uncanny representation of all aspects of the impending crime. As you can see, the house, its contents and the personage of Pip, as the murder victim, have been perfectly reproduced in all details apart from size. However, budget restrictions limit us to a half-scale. This means we can monitor events as they unfold.'

I experienced a surge of anger, 'You mean that you

He held it up to his lips and touched it to his tongue. He turned his head up and closed his eyes as if he had sipped an exquisite nectar.

'Please allow me to rub a little on the troubled skin.'

I was compressed between the kitchen wall and the ceiling and could hardly move.

He thrust himself between my parted legs and started rubbing the dock leaf on my exposed thigh. I could see his hand shaking as it approached my crotch.

'My dear, dear, dear boy.'

I managed to push him backwards and scramble out of the door into the hall. I tried the front door but it wouldn't open. I realised an automatic lock appeared to have been activated. I had no choice but to leap up the stairs.

Mr Peacock followed.

Unfortunately, he managed to catch hold of my foot and I found myself sliding back down the stairs.

'You mustn't resist. I do understand. But if you resist, I fear you may perish.' My shoe and sock came off in his hand and he staggered backwards and fell over next to the front door. I took the opportunity of dashing back up the stairs. I went into the bedroom that knew what was going on. You could have prevented Pip's murder.'

'I see you are an intelligent young man. This makes my job so much easier. So you will understand that this is the crux of the whole matter. This is the very serious problem we face.

'The reputation of the policemen has fallen to an all-time low. They are considered by the public to have a level of moral development no higher than insects. Needless to say that if the body of law enforcement in a society has reached such a point of depravity, then this has an adverse effect of that society. That society will be dragged down to the level of a lower form of life. Human relationships indeed have declined. Natural birth has ceased. Nipples have gone missing. As you know from your own case, belly buttons can mysteriously disappear. The entire mammalian project is in tatters. We now have mummyhood deprived of mummies and daddyhood deprived of daddies. Babyhood deprived of real babies. What is left? Here at the Independent Police Complaints Commission, we consider this to be an act of was the equivalent of the one used by my brother and me.

I sat down with my back against the door. In no time Mr Peacock was calling through the door.

'I'm sorry. I meant you no harm. I didn't realise how you were feeling. Can I come in and apologise? Please. Like good men we can make amends. Come, let us shake hands and put this minor misapprehension behind us.'

I wasn't falling for that one. The door started to inch open. Despite the pressure I was exerting, I began to slide along the floor. Despite increasing my efforts to keep him out, the door had opened sufficiently for Mr Peacock to poke his head round.

'Go on. Let me in.'

I didn't have much choice. He'd completely pushed open the door. As he walked forward, I backed towards the wall. It reached a point that I could go no further.

'I can see that you're very unhappy. We can only be made whole by opening up to what is deep inside. Don't repress anything. Be careful how you assess this situation. Don't be fooled into thinking that our freedom lies in the control of our desires by the rational mind.

theft committed by the policemen themselves.

'That isn't the end of the matter. Naturally the policemen are seeking to re-establish their reputations. They are working to win back the public's regard and affection by reinstating their humanity. I'm afraid this is being achieved by the policemen having ruthlessly initiated a crime wave of monstrous proportions that has the public in the grip of unendurable panic. To cope with the crime of their own instigation, they have drastically increased their numbers by some means of asexual reproduction. Likely this is similar to parthenogenesis, the mode of reproduction favoured by the aphids and such. When they successfully stem the crime wave. they believe they will restore the public's confidence in them.

The Independent Police Complaints Commission holds that the way back to public confidence is through the device of the policemen's integrity. We have formed the opinion that the system of evaluation must be completely separate from the system of motivation. Evaluation must be made in a cool, calm, non-

'Reason exists only to secure our desires. Great philosophers in the empiricist camp concur on this point. I refer of course to Hume's 'Enquiries'. I can reassure you that Kant's 'Groundwork of the Metaphysics of Morals', is a floored, misconceived work. I implore you to abandon any commitment to this work.

'I must admit at this point that this replica has been built by the Police Complaints Commission but it is not for the purpose of investigating the police activities surrounding Pip's murder at all. It has been built to simply fulfil your dreams. Perhaps you don't realise that yet. I assure you that it will equally fulfil mine. But I think deep down you know what you really want.'

There was no way out. The only space to the outside was the half-scale head-hole of my brother in the window.

Just as I thought there was no hope for me, an ichneumon fly unexpectedly flew through the head-hole.

It landed on Mr Peacock's nose. I took advantage of his distraction and whacked his hooter as hard as I could. It left the flattened creature dangling from the end of his nose, as blood suddenly

self-deceptive moment. These moments can only be provided by the IPCC. Only we can keep in check the policemen's primordial desires. This is surely the means to regain our stature as civilised creatures.

The policemen disagree. Quite to the contrary of our opinion, they have outlawed us and currently we are on the run. They hope to hunt us down and exterminate us. It is imperative that you keep our presence a secret. If you can keep us informed as to the exact goings on of the policemen, then I'm sure we can resolve the matter. We must bring the whole sordid affair to the attention of the public.'

An ichneumon fly unexpectedly entered the kitchen from the hall and landed on Mr Peacock's nose. He became quite agitated

'What is it? Get it off. Get it off.'

He was shaking his hands frantically but to little effect.

Mr Peacock's complexion turned white in panic at the insect's presence. It seemed up to me to do something. Without thinking I whacked the ichneumon fly with my fist. I'd forgotten about the presence of Mr Peacock's nose. Mr Peacock looked at me, erupted from one of the nostrils.

I took the opportunity to escape.

I dashed back down the stairs, quickly picking up the shoe and sock lying at the bottom.

Then I scrambled through the kitchen door to the comparative safety of the embankment.

startled by my action, as blood suddenly erupted from one of his nostrils and trickled to the top of his lip.

I was quite frightened by what I'd done. I really had no reason to hurt Mr Peacock.

Without pausing, I hastily scrambled through the kitchen door and out to the comparative safety of the embankment.

6. Pip's Ghost

I was in deep confusion.

I wasn't sure if I'd just tried to defend somebody or attack them. Whether I'd been helped or violated.

The one thing I can be absolutely certain of is that I left Mr Peacock nursing a bleeding nose and a crushed ichneumon fly.

By now I was used to hiding till it was dark. When I felt safe from the police, I climbed back up to Pip's house. Certainly the police car had gone.

I found the house forbidding. There were no lights on and it appeared to be deserted.

I peered through the window and could just make out the unmoving figure of my brother sitting in Beatrice's chair opposite Pip's chair. I knocked on the window but he didn't respond. Had it reached that critical point in a murder investigation when another victim is about to be discovered?

Was it going to be my brother? I went to the front door. It was half open, hanging off its hinges.

I entered the house, filled with dread. I tried to switch on the light but the bulbs had been removed. I went into the living room and sat down opposite my static brother. In the partial light of the streetlights my brother raised his hand a couple of inches and wiggled his fingers at me in a greeting.

He was not in good shape.

Even in the semi-darkness I could see they'd peeled tissue from his eyes and ears for the police examination. His tongue was blackened from the promised drilling, causing his voice to be thick and distorted.

I noticed the forensic experts had done a thorough job on the house. Most of the decent furniture had been removed, including the curtains and carpets. In fact pretty much all that was left was Pip and Beatrice's chairs. The fridge had been emptied apart from a half-filled bottle of rancid milk at the back and a mouldy mince pie from last Christmas. There wasn't a single sheet of toilet paper left. All the jam had gone, leaving the cupboard bare.

'Why have they let you go?'

'I really don't know. I think they're still amassing evidence. It's only a matter of time before they come back for me.'

It didn't seem good.

Sitting in the darkness I suddenly noticed something that was unavailable to me before. Entirely consistent with Pip's system of belief, I realised his geist was still here in the house. Clearly the energy that he'd accumulated in his productive life was unspent when he died. It was incredibly faint but I could just make it out in his chair, like spotting a nebula with the naked eye. The trick was to not look directly at Pip's geist but to look slightly to one side and receive the faint image on the most sensitive part of the retina.

My brother's senses were too impaired to detect him. However, I felt he intuitively knew he was there because he'd chosen to sit in Beatrice's chair rather than Pip's.

As I focussed on the image I realised I could just make out a faint sound like wind rustling the autumn leaves.

I could see that Pip's lips were moving but I could not make out what he was saying. Ingeniously I took a seashell from the hearth and trapped his diminished words in its fragile chamber.

This was madness. Why did the police refuse to apply their advanced technologies to question the ghosts of the dead in order to discover the identity of their murderers? Maybe Mr Peacock was right. Maybe the police were hiding something.

I abstracted Pip's voice from the seashell.

'Boys. Boys, I have been shouting caution at you since my demise. Will nobody listen to me? My ghost is almost spent. That is why I'm so faint. I will soon be gone forever'

'But what happened Pip? What happened to you after you left us to relieve your bladder?'

'My thoughts on the ghost turned out to be almost accurate, for this is the root of the matter. I have a confession, boys. A confession that throws new light on Beatrice's recent behaviour. You see, a long time ago I had an affair with my childhood sweetheart, Verity. This was during the time that I was wed to Beatrice, be it only for a short time. Beatrice found out and threw rages at me. I understand all that. Beatrice insisted that to repair the damage to our understanding, I had to repay her exactly, in precisely defined measures, the pleasure that Verity consumed. Beatrice believed that was rightfully hers. That was why I was involved in a seemingly endless sexual toil even into the extreme of old age. For my affair with Verity was long and passionate. As death threatened to cheat Beatrice of the final payments, so she increased her demand. Naturally I thought I would die first. No doubt you did, going by the constant knocking of the bedpost against the wall. Surprisingly, I was wrong. When her heart stopped beating, our reminiscences were not entirely as cordial as I originally suggested. They also included Verity. When the end came, I think that is why the geist was frustrated and restless. That is why the ghost caused the separated body to rage and trash the bedroom. Why she tried to kill me. She was aware that I still owed her pleasure. When she was laid to rest, I was aware the miserly layer of earth was hardly adequate to contain the gases of putrefaction let alone her torment and anger. Yes, boys, when I took that last piss, it was Beatrice that bore down on me from behind and ended my life. As I piddled on the porcelain, the mirror in the bathroom had steamed up with the vapours that arose from the intensity of urination. I don't know what came over me, boys. With the full awareness that Beatrice had only just been buried, I wrote 'VERITY' on the glass. Then, as I was zipping up, in the parts of the clear mirror revealed by the letters, I saw the familiar figure of Beatrice approaching me with a club. Unmistakably it was Beatrice. I have seen the doings of the police and recognise their corruption. I think you may have guessed that Verity was your natural mother. When she was swelled with the two of you in her womb, the policemen became jealous of her mammalian stature. When she was giving birth, they beat her to death and confiscated the umbilical cord and all the traces of your origin. That is why you lack belly buttons. I was unable to explain the truth to you because of the appalling wrong I did to Beatrice. It was only a matter of time before the police came back for you. You must demonstrate to the police that it was Beatrice, helplessly pathetic and deranged, that performed the murderous act on me. She is not to blame. The fault is entirely mine. Creep now to the cemetery, boys and reveal to the police that her grave is empty and that you are innocent.'

I felt this wasn't quite right.

'But Pip, this does not account for everything. Why was your body not found? Why was there nothing left of you apart from a rather fine portrait in oils? Why was the portrait found in our bedroom when you were beaten to death in the bathroom? What happened to the murder weapon? How did Beatrice escape the grave? And if she did, could her actions be explained by post mortem movements? They seemed to stop at the end of the night we sat in vigil. How can we have been born to Verity at the same time when we are both different ages? We are not twins Pip. We differ in age by two years..........'

'Stop. Stop. How can you doubt the testimony of the geist. It has the particular qualities of clarity and certainty. Is it not pure and unadulterated? Please, I have no time for this, I'm fading. I beg you to dig up Beatrice's grave. It will be empty. Then you can prove you are innocent. The police will have to track her down.'

'But Pip, we are frightened and weak. How can we manage this?'

He must have seen that I was small and terrified. My brother looked crumpled and uncomprehending.

The faint light became even fainter. I could see Pip struggling in anguish. Then suddenly his geist snuffed out and we were left alone.

I sat devastated. So it wasn't Pip it was Pop. Now Pop was gone.

We sat in misery. It was now just a matter of time before the police cars returned and we would no doubt both be charged with the murder of Pip.

And then a miracle happened.

Although Pip's light had gone out I could sense him within me. I could hear him talking to me. His momentum was driving mine. I had become empowered with Pip's geist. The two of us formed a unity. I rose up refreshed and stronger to attempt Pip's suggestion of digging up Beatrice.

We waited till the middle of the night and gathered at the front of the house. My brother was too weak and addled to walk, so I decided to push him in Pip's wheelbarrow. I left him propped against the front gate as I went round the back to find the barrow.

When I returned DI Bosch and Sergeant Callot were both standing next to my brother. I'm sure they'd both been drinking.

'Ah, the tell-tale squeak of the wheelbarrow. So where are you off to, lads? I warn you that the net is closing. In the very near future I fear you will not have the freedom to go squeaking with your wheelbarrow in the middle of the night. Enjoy it while you can. But first we need your assistance. This afternoon the forensics team discovered a body buried in your very own back garden. We request that you accompany us to the police mortuary where you will be required to identify it. I think you appreciate the seriousness of this development and all the implications that it carries.'

DI Bosch stepped forward and pinched my cheek hard like he'd pinched my brother's cheek on our first encounter with him. Our faces became close.

'So, you're the bright one are you? Think you can escape the hornets' nest without a blemish and rise above the system? You are mistaken. All that has happened is that you have drawn attention to yourself. You have made yourself conspicuous. As certainly as we are going to nab your brother, we are going to nab you.'

7. The Police Mortuary

The police car dropped us off outside the police
mortuary. Bosch opened the front door by pushing a plastic
wafer in a slot and keying in his identity.

I gathered Bosch and Callot had other bodies to attend.
I noticed in the mortuary there were no jolly policemen's songs
or comical jigs. They sped off down the corridor giving
garbled instructions as to where we were to go to identify the
body.

My hatred and distrust for them continued to grow.
They seemed too familiar with the mortuary. It seemed well
within their powers to plant a cadaver to fake the evidence
against us.

We navigated the forbidding building. We wandered
up one of the brightly-lit corridors lined on the walls, ceiling
and floor with tiles. The white tiles stank strongly of
antiseptic. Every ten feet, on both sides of the corridor, there
were drains as if the whole building was in a constant struggle
to cleanse itself. There were no windows.

One of the difficulties I was experiencing at this point
of time was the presence of Pip's ghost. Although initially it
was wonderful to be reunited with him, the union was proving
to be a strain. It certainly wasn't the Pip that I remembered.
Having his comprehensive library and precision tools stripped
by the police seemed to have had a reducing effect on him. In
all my memories, he had always been elderly but vigorous. It
was as if I was now dealing with somebody in the early
symptoms of senile decay. I had to provide him with a

constant commentary but he was unable to take it in. Sometimes I did this silently in my head but more often than not I muttered the commentary out loud. He seemed to be unable to grasp where we were or what was happening. Nor did he seem to understand that I couldn't focus on him all the time. I needed to be able to concentrate on what I was doing. Having Pip's ghost within was beginning to prove a handicap.

'No Pip. We are not in the cemetery about to dig Beatrice up. We are not even approaching the cemetery. We got side-tracked by the police. No, we are in the mortuary, Pip. THE POLICE MORTUARY.'

I wasn't getting through. Further, Bosch's instruction bore no resemblance to the building. I suspect he was deliberately trying to arrange it so that we got lost as part of the campaign of intimidation.

Supporting my brother, we staggered up the corridor.

The structure of my brother's legs appeared to collapse as if he had contracted rickets. I left him propped up against a wall. I selected a trolley from several abandoned in a stair well and helped him on to it. I tucked him reassuringly under the blanket and continued our arbitrary journey.

As we passed along the cold corridors I could see through the glass of the doors, arrays of drawers reaching from the floor to the ceiling. They seemed endless. On the outside of each door was a complex of thermostats individually regulating the temperature of the occupants. Every unit I could see appeared to be in operation. I wondered if all these were the victims of unsolved crimes. The sheer weight of the dead began to unnerve me. I started to belt along at full speed, finding it difficult to maintain the trolley on a straight trajectory. Several times it struck the wall.

I still didn't know where I was going and went into a panic. Should I keep going or would it be better to go back? The longer I keep going on the further it is to return. I left it another five minutes on my present course and I came to a halt. I started to whimper and reversed. I may have just been getting tired, but the trolley seemed to be getting much harder to push. With a massive effort I got it to move slowly. It felt like the wheels were hardly turning. It was as if I was trying to push poles of powerful magnets together. I couldn't help feeling this was something to do with the effect of the mortuary on my brother's spent body. The inertia of his body seemed to be increasing.

The lights started to go dim. It must just be this corridor. I pushed the trolley to the next, but it was even dimmer. I was now having difficulty opening the doors at the ends of the corridors. I tried to push the trolley harder and managed to gain a little more speed but the lights went down to a faint red glow. It seemed the harder I pushed the trolley the more the lights dimmed. Finally the door completely jammed and the lights went out completely.

I stood frozen in the total darkness. I could hear a low moaning sound emitting from my brother but I was unable to reassure him. The warning lights on the thermostats turned from green to red and the odour of decay wafted in from the air vents.

Somewhere nearby an alarm bell rang out and I could hear frantic voices shouting in the distance. A figure in a white overall appeared through the darkness with a powerful arc lamp. He called out to a colleague.

'It's alright, I've found the blockage.'

He held the light up to my face and spat contempt.

'You stupid, stupid little boy. Have you no idea where you are? Can't you read? You must have seen the notices. If you push somebody on a trolley they must be either completely dead or completely alive. Isn't it obvious. Are you so stupid that you can't see how dangerous that can be? He's not a 'straight' but neither is he a 'breather'. Look how pale and gaunt he looks. There is barely movement of air in his bronchial passages and a pitiful quantity of blood trickling through his veins. He is obviously virtually dead even though technically he counts as alive. Are you really not aware that there is a delicate ecology precariously balanced in these places? Years of fine tuning can be lost in a single reckless moment like this. Do you think all these lights and refrigeration units run off the national grid? Do you expect us just to be able to put all this right in two seconds?'

His pointing finger jabbed my nose. I tried to apologise but my voice came out in a weak, high-pitched waver. He dragged my brother off the trolley by the collar and to a small degree the lights came back on. He thumped him in the stomach and walked off wheeling the trolley. My brother sank down and curled up on the floor and the lights became slightly brighter. The ventilation system begrudgingly started to clean the air again.

The attendant departing with the trolley partially turned round.

'Follow the corridor to the right over there. Keep going till you reach the lift. Go down two floors and you'll be at the exit. If you're still in the building in five minutes I will come back and beat the shit out of both of you.'

I helped my brother to his feet and followed the direction we had been given.

As soon as the lift door opened at the exit I could hear raucous laughter. DI Bosch and Sergeant Callot were sitting in the reception with empty coffee cups before them and a plate of chocolate biscuits.

'Did you get lost? Did you bugger the whole ecological balance of the mortuary? It all counts as evidence against you.'

Bosch and Callot stood up and we followed them through a door at the back of the room they were sitting in.

The attendant who shouted at us was in the room beyond, standing next to a large trolley with a sheet draped over it.

Astonishingly, he didn't recognise us. He was quite polite and must have assumed we were relatives come to identify a beloved family member.

'I'm sorry if you've been inconvenienced. Some thugs, no doubt on methadone or something similar, got into the building and screwed up the entire system.

He pulled back the sheet.

There lay Timmy the crab. Small and decayed but still recognisable.

DI Bosch directly addressed me rather than my brother.

'Do you recognise this poor abused creature?'

I couldn't pretend otherwise. My affirmation took the form of a loud sob.

'I'm sorry can you speak a little clearer? Do you or do you not recognise this poor abused creature'?

"YES. ITS. TIMMY. THE. CRAB."

'Forensic tests reveal this small crustacean was effectively tortured to death and was then carried some distance from its natural homeland and placed in a shallow grave. That shallow grave was in your own back garden or are you prepared to deny this fact against all the evidence? Was it you that buried Timmy?

I nodded, unable to speak. I had been unable to leave Timmy where he had fallen so I hid him in a lollipop wrapper and took him home. Eventually the smell started to attract the attention of Beatrice so I was forced to bury Timmy in the back garden.

'Do you deny this is the beginning of a slippery slope? It is the body of one small, insignificant creature today but who is to say what will happen tomorrow? Will there be another body of human proportions next time? And then another. And another until we have the work of a serial murderer on our hands.'

DI Bosch delicately picked Timmy up by one of his legs and held him under my nose. I flinched and tried to move away but Sergeant Callot constrained me.

'So where is Pip? Is it you that have hidden him? Is he about to turn up in similar sordid circumstances as Timmy?'

He tapped a finger hard on my forehead and grinned.

'He's not in there is he? Do you think you've got him safely hidden where nobody can find him? How are you working this one? Is it division of labour? Maybe your brother provides the bodies and you bury them? Even if he's up there somewhere in your head it doesn't mean it isn't a murder. Be warned. In this case there may be no geistless-body but a bodiless-geist secreted in the nervous system is no less evidence that a heinous crime has been committed.'

The smell of poor Timmy started to make me wretch. DI Bosch held him a moment longer than necessary beneath my nostrils and then flung him in the dustbin in the corner. Timmy's exoskeleton fragmented on the metallic rim of the bin and the individual bits fell into the black plastic liner containing a mass of other disposed body parts.

'So, merry lads, it's back to your little frolic in the dark involving a wheelbarrow. But as we like to say, pieces of the jigsaw puzzle are fitting together. Enjoy your little frolic when you can lads, because time is running out.'

8. The Nettle Eaters

The police car dropped us once again outside Pip's house. I waited until it had driven off again before collecting a torch and my red plastic bucket and seaside spade. I bundled my brother into the wheelbarrow and set off for the cemetery.

We passed through the allotments at the side of the embankment. Black steam engines passed up and down ceaselessly, throwing demonic fire to the overcast sky. I must admit I wasn't looking forward to this.

I still had Pip's geist twittering interminably in my head. I suppose the whole trouble was that he didn't know what was happening. He couldn't see or hear anything and I had to constantly explain what was happening.

'No Pip, we're not in the morgue anymore. We're going along the allotments to the cemetery to dig Beatrice up.'

The recent events of Beatrice's death and his own murder had certainly wrecked his peace of mind. If he ever had peace of mind.

I opened the squeaky gate that led into the back of the cemetery and we approached Beatrice's grave.

So I simply started digging with my seaside spade. Down and down with my brother largely inert, muttering to himself beside the grave and Pip rattling away in my head.

I tried to blot it all out and find reassurance by singing rousing hymns

And did those feet in ancient times,
Walk upon England's pastures green.

Eventually my frail little spade hit the surface of the coffin. I dug round it and shone my torch on to the lid. There was no damage to it. I'd swear that nobody had got in or out of it. Beatrice was definitely still inside. I didn't know how to tell Pip.

Pip started up again, but it was to be the last time.

'See boys, she's not there. Look for yourselves. This is the proof that she is my murderer. Her body is still aquiver for vengeance. She long ago escaped the coffin, probably before she was buried. It is that that proved my undoing. Come on, boys. Demonstrate this one fact, that the coffin is empty and you can prove your own innocence.'

Very well. I sliced under the lid until it loosened.

The clouds parted and revealed the newly created black sky crammed tight with spinning galaxies and planetary bodies. Our ears filled with their gentle but eerie hissing.

The lid creaked open and I climbed out of the pit.

What can I say Pip? I'm so sorry.

Beatrice was simply lying there. There she was, completely still in the shadows.

Everything suddenly went very quiet inside.

Pip's voice was silenced. In fact he never spoke again. It was as if the contradiction with his earlier testimony had simply deleted his geist. He had been so certain. I did feel a stab of loss, but I felt it was for the best. He couldn't have gone on like that.

I looked down at Beatrice and suddenly felt frightened as to what we might be releasing. I made a scramble to replace the coffin lid and fill the hole in.

I was too late.

Beatrice flew at us. Not with a hidden weapon or any particular malice. There was a frantic tearing of pupae and she dispersed into a cloud of peacock butterflies. Her familiar form held for a second or two before spreading like a cloud in the night sky. Against the starry sky my brother and I saw the cloud of butterflies meander to the railway embankment at the edge of the cemetery and merge with the stinging nettles that would provide nutrition for their offspring.

For a moment we were gobsmacked. Then my virtually disabled brother rose to his feet and sped from the cemetery, back through the allotments by the embankment and towards our house. I paused a second or two more trying to take in what had happened. Then I ran after him, leaving behind a large pile of soil and a hole with an empty coffin at the bottom. Next to the hole was a red plastic bucket, a seaside spade and a wheelbarrow, all liberally spattered with my fingerprints.

We lay side by side in our bleak, inhospitable house in the positions our beds would have been if not for this current crisis. The floor was hard and there were no blankets. I felt cold and miserable.

My brother entered a deep, peaceful sleep as soon as we returned. Maybe he was exhausted. In the circumstances I was unable to relax. I was still awake trying to make sense of what had happened. The sky started to brighten in the east.

What did it mean that Beatrice was butterflies? Had she always been butterflies and we just didn't realise it.? Or more likely, was it that she was pupae?

I couldn't lie there any more. I went over to the window. The sun was about to rise above the horizon.

I noticed in the corner of the room a little bloody pile of tissue that had issued from my brother's eye when we were having the fight over belly buttons. I was surprised that the forensic team that had stripped the house down after Pip's murder had failed to remove it for analysis.

On the outside it had dried but when I poked it with a pencil I found it was still moist inside. I pulled out the pencil and dangling from the end was the lens. It was still in working order because when I held it up to the window it transmitted to the wall an inverted image of the view of the rising sun.

I stood before the mirror on the wall above the sink and peered through the lens at my own eye. The pupil revealed a black impenetrable aperture. The rising sun rose to a specific angle that cast an orange shaft directly through the pupil. All became illuminated. Deep inside, I could see the restless configuration and reconfiguration of what looked like a colony of insects in an uncomprehending toil. They shimmered and shifted until the angle of the sun altered and the aperture snapped back into darkness.

Was this the source of my movements. Like Beatrice, was I a nettle eater?

I needed advice. But where might I find it? Certainly not the police. Depending on which aspect of Mr Peacock's account you believed, they were the cause of the crime in the first place. There didn't seem to be much choice. The only person I could seek advice from was Mr Peacock himself.

I looked at my brother sleeping. He seemed so peaceful so I didn't wake him.

By the time the sun had fully risen and was warming the east wall of the house, I'd left the house and was climbing the railway embankment back to Mr Peacock's odd little household.

My second encounter with Mr Peacock was more confusing than the first and again I have had to divide my account into two columns in order to make any sense of what happened.

9. Mrs Peacock

Nervously I tapped on the door.
It opened two centimetres and I could see Mr Peacock's eye through the gap. The door was on one of those chains that stop it opening altogether. This was different from Pip's house, which had no such device.

Nervously I tapped on the door.
It opened two centimetres and I could see Mr Peacock's eye through the gap. The door was on one of those chains that stop it opening altogether. This was different from Pip's house, which had no such device. When he saw who it

When he saw who it was, Mr Peacock opened the door as far as the chain would stretch. I noticed he wasn't too keen for me to come in this time. His nose was dressed with a large bulbous bandage attached to his cheeks with Elastoplast. The door closed. There was muttering behind the door as if he was debating with himself as to what to do. I could hear the chain being unfastened. The door opened fully this time.

'My dear, dear boy. What can I say? The last time we seemed to get our wires crossed. The fault is entirely mine. Please, please, come in. Let's make a fresh start.' Reluctantly I agreed. I had hoped to make this transaction on the doorstep. But his frank apology changed the balance of things. I squeezed into the hall and followed Mr Peacock into the kitchen.

'So you want some advice from me. If there's one piece of advice I can give you, whichever way you are inclined, it is always to have a packet of condoms on your person at any time. You never know what is about to happen. See, I have one here.'

was, Mr Peacock opened the door as far as the chain would stretch. I noticed he wasn't too keen for me to come in this time. His nose was dressed with a large bulbous bandage attached to his cheek with Elastoplast. The door closed. There was a muttering behind the door as if he was debating with himself as to what to do. I could hear the chain being unfastened. The door opened fully this time.

'My dear, dear boy. What can I say? What happened last time was my own fault. You see, I have a not altogether irrational fear of the ichneumon fly. All the same, I'm sorry I panicked. I know it alarmed you and when you whopped me on the snoz, you thought you'd done something wrong. Let me assure you. You were absolutely right to do what you did. You had to save me from the ichneumon fly. Please come into the kitchen and make yourself as comfortable as possible.'

I squeezed my way through the hall to the kitchen.

With perfect accuracy, Mr Peacock anticipated all that happened from the resurrection and extinction of Pip's geist, to the identification of Timmy the crab's body at the morgue. He was aware

Mr Peacock scrambled with difficulty in the limited space into his back pocket. He removed a small cardboard box. He opened it and took out a condom in a little cellophane wrapper.

'Take it. Keep it with you at all times. Don't worry, I have plenty more.'

Dubiously I accepted his present and put it in my pocket.

'Really, in these troublesome days it could be a life-saver.'

I thanked him for his advice.

'Now, would you like a glass of lemonade?'

'Not really. I'm OK thanks.'

'No, go on. I insist. After what you've been through.'

He leaned to one side and opened the back kitchen door. From what would have been the scullery in Pip's house he produced a full-size glass and an apparently unopened bottle of lemonade.

He poured it into the glass and passed it to me.

'If you don't mind, I'll just pop to the bathroom.'

I listened to him going up the stairs. I put the glass to my lips and noticed that it didn't smell quite right.

that Beatrice was butterflies. Mr Peacock nodded his head wisely.

'Indeed, these are troubling times. But the fact that Beatrice is butterflies does not necessarily imply that Beatrice is the murderer as Pip thought. Anybody who observes a butterfly in their back garden knows that they are random, harmless creatures and are unlikely to be capable of calculated murder. However, many butterflies appear in your garden on a summer's day, it hardly poses a physical threat. As we have already discussed, the Police Complaints Commission maintains the police themselves are at the root of this. Some people dismiss this, saying that it is fundamentally the purpose of the Police Complaints Commission to place unjustified criticism on the policemen.

'That is not the case. We have made very careful investigations and have come up with some very disturbing facts.

'The police records reveal for instance that Bosch's training as a detective required him to become a highly qualified painter with a marked ability at unusual composition. Although

I poured it down the miniature kitchen sink and waited. Mr Peacock returned to the kitchen. He was no longer wearing any trousers.

My heart sank. Mr Peacock looked at my empty glass.

'Ah, good man. You must have been thirsty after all. Are you feeling relaxed? There's nothing wrong is there?'

'I noticed that my drink tasted funny, so I poured it down the sink'

'No. Really, no. What are you saying? That I put something naughty in your drink? How outrageous. You're getting all muddled again, like you did last time. It isn't like that at all.'

He was blocking the back door.

As I'd feared, we were going through all that again.

I pulled myself hastily out of the kitchen and toward the front door.

The automatic lock had been activated as before.

Suddenly I was in a passionate clinch with Mr Peacock.

'Really, you're taking this the wrong way. Come up stairs and lie on the bed where it's much comfier and we'll talk it through. We

Callot's medium is mainly lithography, his style is nonetheless acknowledged to be inspired by Bosch's. Might this not go some way to explain the portraiture found at the alleged scene of Pip's demise? You noticed that the window was open. When the murderous act was done, who is to say that the long arm of the law didn't place the portrait in the room afterwards?

"We are currently investigating the goings on at the police headquarters itself. In fact, at any moment, I'm expecting a report from my colleague who goes under the pseudonym of Mrs Peacock. We believe that Dr Baker, the head of the forensic team, is extending the facility of DNA analysis far beyond its conventional application. Of course, the most important use of DNA analysis is in the solving of old crimes where the suspects and witnesses are long dead. It is well known that the forensic team bring back the principal suspects using cloning techniques. If they are found to be guilty, in a fair trial, they are exposed to the outrage of the public who take summary revenge by flaying them by the most barbaric means imaginable.

could take our clothes off, then we'd be much more relaxed. What do you say to that?'

I wasn't that enthusiastic.

I knew the back door was open so I shoved him hard to one side and pushed my way back to the kitchen.

Just as I was crawling through the kitchen I felt a heavy weight fall on me and I went down flat on my face. Mr Peacock was lying directly on top of me.

'See what happens when you rudely refuse to accept your host's hospitality. You have to be tied up and shown the proper way to behave.'

I was pinned down with my hands yanked behind me and his knee in the small of my back. I couldn't move. Rope was already in his hand and he was expertly tying my wrists together.

'And now. As luck would have it, Private Pinkie is standing to attention and I believe it is time for you both to become better acquainted.'

The back door unexpectedly opened and a formidable looking woman was staring imperiously at us through the aperture.

'Really, what on earth do you think you are doing, Clive?'

All this of course in strict proportion to the severity of the crime. We believe that Dr Baker has gone beyond his brief.'

The back door unexpectedly opened and a formidable looking woman was staring imperiously at us through the aperture.

Mr Peacock introduced us.

'This is Mrs Peacock. This is the colleague whose report I've been expecting. I must explain. When it's Mrs, she pretending to be my wife. However, in some circumstances, we find it necessary to pretend she is my sister in which case we use the title Miss. In having two pseudonyms there is always the risk that dangerous mistakes can be made.'

I suddenly had a sense of longing behind Mr Peacock's dry, academic composure. I suspected that in other circumstances he would have been pleased to introduce Mrs Peacock as his real wife. I imagined him hoping their relationship would change once the long standing conflict between the police and the Complaints Commission had finally been resolved.

Mrs Peacock removed papers from her brief case that confirmed that Dr Baker's

Mr Peacock seemed disoriented and felt the need to introduce us.

'Ah. Yes. This is my wife, Miss Peacock. I mean this is my sister Mrs Peacock. Bollocks, bollocks, bollocks. Let me assure you before you point the accusing finger, we have never committed any act of incest or similar in this house.'

I assumed the cavalry had arrived and I was saved but I don't know why exactly.

'So you've got the boy again and you're going ahead on your own I see. You hog everything. Well, you're not getting away with it again, Clive. You selfish little turd. I'm coming in on this one. And if you think I'm doing it on the kitchen floor like an animal you're mistaken. Get him upstairs.'

Mr Peacock dragged me to my feet and pushed me along the hall and then upstairs. Now that I was on my feet, I could feel the rope round my wrists loosen. I kept my hands clasped behind my back. Mr Peacock threw me onto the bed. Mrs Peacock followed us into the room.

'So what are you intending to do with him when we've finished fucking him?'

DNA experiments were at the heart of the problem.

'The unusual direction that Dr Baker's research has taken is to modify the DNA of parasitic wasps.

'Basically, parasitic wasps are solitary predators that do not live in the ordered hives as do other species of wasps. Why has he done this? Why has he gone beyond his contractual obligation to further crime detection in order to commit this apparently charitable act of freeing the parasitic wasp from a life of interminable solitude? We have our suspicions and I think the implication is stark for humankind.'

I didn't know what she meant by this. It certainly had a devastating effect on Mr Peacock. He buried his face in his hands and wept copiously.

There was an embarrassing silence so I piped up.

'What do you think I should do?'

'What do I think you should do? I don't know. Pour petrol on the whole thing and then drop a match on it. Become a suicide bomber. Maybe it would be better to develop a weapon of mass destruction and have done with the whole thing. How am

A small disagreement arose.

Mr Peacock thought that I should be cut cleanly in half and left at either side of the embankment. Mrs Peacock displayed contempt.

'Why kill him when he contains virtually an inexhaustible supply of valuable secretions. We can keep him here as a prisoner.'

But Mr Peacock was worried that it might alert the attention of DI Bosch and Sergeant Callot.

'For Christ's sake if we kill him it most certainly will attract Bosch and Callot's attention. Especially with your absurd scheme.'

The dispute between them turned into a full-blown row. Mr Peacock claimed he had more experience dealing with these matters. Mrs Peacock tore the bandage off Mr Peacock's nose. The nose was badly swollen and it started bleeding again.

'If you are so bloody experienced, how did you get that?'

Then they did the thing of putting their faces close together and spitting bitter contempt, their heads wagging from side to side. They became completely I supposed to know what you should do?'

The bandage on his nose began to unravel in a snotty tangle.

'You were no doubt taught at school that history is the kings and queens. Marx said it was the class struggle. Now Mrs Peacock is saying that it is the butterflies and parasitic wasps.'

Mrs Peacock became angry with him.

'You really are becoming a defeatist Clive. The boy asks a reasonable question and you turn wet all of a sudden. What's got into you this morning?'

Mr Peacock started to cry again.

'What am I supposed to say? The policemen always anticipate our next move. It's become a race that we're losing. In the pernicious application of forensic science they are mocking and stripping all that is human in us. And I know at the end of it all, after they've plundered and demoralised us, they will no doubt celebrate their triumph by displaying themselves as a vulgar parody of humanity.'

Mrs Peacock's anger subsided and she squeezed into the confined space and oblivious as to what was happening about them.

So I carefully slid from the bed and managed to wrench the constraining ropes from my wrists.

Without their noticing, I crept from their tiny house through the back door and made my way home.

embraced Mr Peacock. They wept together in the full knowledge that the machinations of the police were about to deprive them of all future happiness.

Without their noticing, I crept from their tiny house through the back door and made my way home.

10. Petrol

If I'm honest, I suggest the Police Complaints Commission are losing it a bit.

I reflected on the confusing advice I'd been given by Mr Peacock and tried to stitch it all together in the most plausible way that may be useful to my situation.

It was all a bit meagre.

1. Always carry a condom

2. Build a weapon of mass destruction.

I think that adequately sums it all up.

I removed the condom Mr Peacock had given me from its cellophane wrapper and gave it all some thought.

I went to Pip's shed at the bottom of the garden. I took down the can of petrol that he used for the mower and carefully filled the condom. It swelled out magnificently into a giant, unstable sausage. I wondered if the petrol might erode the material of the condom, so I held it up to the light for several moments. It didn't seem to be leaking, so I tied up the end with garden twine. I pulled up the left leg of my trousers and strapped it on just above the knee. I pondered it for a moment. It felt as if an enormous inflammable carbuncle with unusual refractive properties had suddenly erupted on my leg. I carefully poked its cool, stretched exterior to check it was OK and then pulled down my trouser leg. I picked up Pip's bonfire matches and struck one to see if they were still operable. I then made sure they were in my pocket at all times.

I went back to Pip's gutted house. My brother was still sleeping peacefully. I took my place next to him. Maybe I did feel a little better after Mr Peacock's advice because for the first time for quite a long time I felt relaxed enough to sleep. Since we were united as the BROTHERS OF THE LOST BELLY BUTTON I found, once I was asleep, that I had no difficulty slipping into his dream. In fact my brother was waiting for me when I entered.

11. Verity

My brother was younger and he had regained his lost eye.

'Do you see what is happening?'

I didn't immediately.

'Where we are now, time is passing backwards.'

Since he arrived earlier than me he had lost two years. We were now the same age. I had always thought we were quite different in appearance. I realise now that we are identical.

I looked around me. The houses and the railway embankment had gone. I presumed they hadn't been built yet and that we were in the past. We were walking in woodland.

'Don't you see where we're going?

I didn't.

'We're going to meet Verity. Our mother.'

I automatically felt my navel. The belly button had returned. It was still small, but it was growing all the time.

'In the other place death was inevitable. Bosch and Callot were simply out to destroy us both. We're not facing cold extinction here. We're going back to the womb. Which would you prefer? Both are strictly bounded. In the other place we will die, presumably at the hands of the police and that is the end of the matter. In this place we return to our birth and gestation. Then we disperse at conception. I prefer this place.'

I had to agree. In the mammalian dream, this way round made a lot more sense. Instead of the savage, impersonal disintegration that occurs with increasing age and death. We can look forward to an approaching unity with Mama. This would be a gentle dissolution, cell by cell, in the warm uterine ocean.

We set a steady pace through the ancient woodland.

I thought I saw the metallic glint through the trees of a police car moving parallel to us. We increased our pace.

We left the woodland behind and started to walk through a wide valley following the meandering stream at the bottom. In the distance I saw the sea like a strip of clear blue Sellotape on the horizon. It revealed no details but merely its presence in the distance caused me to draw an involuntary breath.

As we got nearer the details of waves and rock started to emerge.

I suddenly realised that Timmy may have been somewhere around. That is Timmy in an earlier phase of evolution when he was living his unadulterated life among the rock pools and sand dunes. He was far away from the inane seaside crowds that would be his undoing. I would have loved to have spent time looking for him but I could see police cars were amassing on the headland. As we approached the point of birth we were getting smaller. Our little legs were running like the clappers.

Where the valley met the coast we turned a corner and there was Verity waiting for us. She was huge and beautiful, towering above us. Her legs were splayed like those of a lover, except that her abdomen was swelling to greet us. From our belly buttons, now fully-grown, protruded the little spikes of umbilical cords. Though I feared the police, I sensed a momentum building up. The ocean started to be drawn into Verity's birth canal producing a powerful undertow. It twisted and opened into a clockwise vortex.

My brother and I stepped into the tide and prepared ourselves for the surge of water. It came quickly and it was warm. The powerful currents dragged us down and down. Our hands were clenched together. We felt no fear of drowning. The umbilical cords made a connection deep within Verity. It reached to the womb. We no longer needed to breathe and we swam in pure joy.

Just for a second the water split above us.

We looked up at Verity and could see her smiling at us.

A bullet from a police sniper ripped into her throat and she went down on to her side.

Time came to a violent halt as if a brake had been slammed on. It then went into a sickening reverse and reoriented again towards death. The warm currents that were drawing us into Verity now spat us into the icy currents of the regular ocean. The umbilical cords retracted and I found I needed to take breath. Salt water burst into my mouth and partially down my gullet, tearing at its lining. My lungs chilled and became solid. I couldn't breathe in and I couldn't breathe out. I thrashed helplessly in the water until I felt my brother's arm around my shoulder dragging me towards the shore.

We lay side by side between the green slimy rocks both choking and retching.

Behind us, uniformed police officers swarmed all over Verity.

Verity, barely alive, was dragged across the beach by the hordes and up towards the headland. There she was tied up with ropes and taken to the bleak moors in the distance.

I followed with a pathetic shambling gait but I was unable to catch up. The distance between us grew. On the moors the policemen beat from her whatever life was left and abandoned the body high up on a hillside.

I straggled far behind. When I got to where Verity was lying, the police had long gone. Little sticky droplets on the red leaves of sundew plants, growing in the sphagnum moss on the hillside, attached to her body and began to dissolve her flesh. Time was now moving forward with disturbing rapidity. Verity's remains sank into moss. The water draining beneath decalcified her bones as the policemen planned. I plunged my hands into the wet moss but I could find nothing.

But where was my brother? I looked back to the distant shore. I could see the swarm of policemen pursuing a tiny figure in the opposite direction. He was now far beyond my reach. The policemen converged on him but I couldn't see exactly what was happening. They pushed him into a police car and it drove off into the distance.

I immediately woke up.

It was dark and the space next to me was empty. I thought I could hear footsteps running up the path.

I quickly got to my feet and ran out of the house to the bottom of the garden.

I could just make out the figure of my brother standing on the railway embankment. I scrambled up and joined him standing on one of the lines. A steam engine was likely to come at any time. I begged him to come down.

'It's useless. They've won.'

'It doesn't have to be like that. We can go back to the dream. To Verity. We can anticipate the police intervention. Adjust our actions. We only just missed it. We were almost there. We can do it next time.'

'I'm stopping it here. The man at the morgue knew what was going to happen to me. There isn't any escape.'

The line was starting to hum but I wasn't sure which way the train was coming.

'Come down now. It isn't too late. We can still fix it.'

'No, you must go.'

'And leave me to face it all alone.'

This seemed to make my brother waver.

'You don't understand. I did kill Pip. I don't know why. It just happened. When you were sleeping I crept upstairs. Pip wasn't in the bathroom. He'd finished his piss and was standing in our bedroom looking mournfully out to the world through the head-hole in the window. Then I did him. Or we did him. Me and the swarm. First we stung his tongue to silence him. Then we stung his eyes to blind him. When you saw him in your dream he wasn't waving, he was flapping wasps. We stung him and stung him till he fell into a hoard of panicking butterflies. We suspected that each might carry copies of Pip's geist and may reconstitute him at some point in the future. So we set on each butterfly and stung it to death. In the end all that was left of Pip was a heap of dead butterflies. A handful at a time, I cast them through the window and they were carried away on the breeze. There was simply nothing left.'

I didn't know what he was talking about.

'Look, whatever happened it was due to the police. It wasn't your fault.'

Behind my brother I could see a patch of darkness expanding, swallowing the city lights. I lunged forward and tried to grab him and topple him down the embankment.

I failed to budge him. The train loomed with its fires suddenly illuminating the embankment. It let out an inhuman scream.

Just before it hit my brother he picked me up bodily and threw me down the side. The train struck my brother and he burst into a cloud of butterflies.

I experienced disbelief of the finality of my brother's end. Surely it wasn't too late to do something. I could still attract the dissipating butterflies with strawberry jam. I could stick them back together with treacle in some reasonable resemblance of my brother. But before my speculations on the matter were completed another train smashed into the butterflies. Their wings fragmented and bodies burst with the violence of the collision. This time the only remnant of my brother was a swarm of Dr Baker's parasitic wasps hanging in the air menacingly. I knew for certain that at this point my brother was dead.

As with the butterflies, the parasitic wasps more or less maintained my brother's shape, albeit more extended and spread out. I felt frightened that they would turn on me and sting me to oblivion as presumably they had done with Pip.

For a few seconds they hovered round me as if weighing up whether to attack. Then suddenly the swarm set off down the embankment. The swarm still maintained my brother's outline as if he was running in slow motion.

Keeping a distance, I followed. The swarm sauntered through the cemetery and along the lanes towards the edge of the city. It was still dark as I followed it through woodland and glades. I walked along bridle paths, rough tracks and lanes until the swarm stopped under the same oak tree that I'd fallen out of when I was escaping from the police headquarters. The shape of my brother stood beneath the tree for a moment before appearing to evaporate in a meandering vapour which was drawn into the papery nest high above the ground.

This seemed to be the best time to try out my hidden weapon.

I untied the condom filled with petrol. I took a piece of the garden twine that I'd used to fasten the condom to my leg and pushed it through the constricted end of the condom so that the petrol soaked into it. I struck one of Pip's matches and lit the fuse. I quickly took aim and then lobbed it at the nest. The flame flapped in the moving air as the bomb flew upward. I knew I was risking it. The thing might miss the nest and fall back on me and set me on fire.

The flame went out. Luckily it missed its target which would have caused it to burst. I managed to catch it without it being ruptured. I pulled the wick out further and lit it again. I had a couple more failures. By my fourth attempt, my eye was better trained and this time, when I lobbed it, it struck the nest. The condom burst and the whole thing went up in flames. I quickly ran from underneath as a spray of burning petrol was ejected from the nest.

I wasn't sure what was going to happen next. I wondered if I'd be enveloped in a swarm of murderous wasps. I could see the nest was burning. At first it burnt with a pale, almost invisible flame. I could hear a sort of muttering sound from within. I expected to see the wasps escaping in droves at any second. The pale flames turned to more substantial yellow flames and the outside layers of the nest peeled off and floated to the ground in virtually weightless flakes.

Thick black smoke started to push out from the top of the nest.

I heard the sorrowful wail of thousands of overlapping voices, then the nest exploded like a roman candle. For several minutes the citizens within were sprayed outwards in a magnificent display of burning wings and carcases.

Eventually it died down into a black smouldering orb and dropped out of the tree. On the ground it collapsed and split. I opened it up with the toe of my shoe. Threads of orange flames on the edges of the ashen laminae flared in the breeze. The nest was definitely dead.

When I reached home it was daylight. I couldn't wait to tell Mr Peacock of my triumph. But as I approached the embankment I could see a trail of smoke. When I approached Mr Peacock's house I could see that it had been gutted by fire. It was as if it had been updated to resemble Pip's house after the police ransacked it for evidence of his murder.

I couldn't see any sign of Mr Peacock or Mrs Peacock.

I went back to Pip's. There wasn't anywhere else to go. I went upstairs to the bedroom I'd recently shared with my brother. Deprived of family and belly button, I waited for the police to come.

As on the day of Pip's murder, the police arrived in force. I could hear shouting as armed officers were deployed to strategic positions. I could hear the machinery of the police gantry delivering Bosch and Callot to the point of final arrest.

The door in front of me burst open and Bosch made an official caution using the one-way of the megaphone.

> **Things don't seem to be going your way anymore do they? If you come quietly and admit your guilt now the court will be more lenient. The evidence is stacked up against you. Although we still have no proof that you disposed of Pip's body after your brother murdered him, you were pretty nifty with the red bucket and seaside spade which we found next to the site of yet another missing body, namely that of Beatrice. You were clearly in league with your brother all along. We haven't even begun investigation of the fate of the individual known as 'Timmy the Crab' and the extent to which you were involved in his premature death.**

There's also the question of lewd behaviour of a specifically sexual nature involving a Mr and Mrs Peacock in the offices of the Police Complaints Commission. The penalty for this is high. We are also taking into account several incidents of arson including the destruction of the office of the Police Complaints Commission and precious woodland in a nearby nature reserve. Traces of petrol found at these sites matched petrol we found stored in Pip's shed. I should add that Mr and Mrs Peacock have been reported missing. Two bodies have been found in the locality and we expect at any moment official confirmation that these are the remains of Mr and Mrs Peacock. Foul play is suspected and you are the only suspect. You see, you were too late. Your pyrolytic activities were mistimed. We've moved on. We've already been promoted for our service to the police and humankind. It's Superintendent Bosch and Detective Inspector Callot now. You're the last of a dying breed. You're the last of the geist-driven nettle eaters. If you are found guilty, and you will be, you will be subject to treatment in the form of our unique brand of insemination. But we don't want you going away with the impression that DI Callot and myself are anything but big-hearted human beings just doing our jobs, we'd like to dance a merry, comical dance just for you.

The police gantry was lowered and Bosch and Callot, once again, adjusted their braces until their trousers were tightly drawn into their groins and the cracks of their arses. As before, they performed a fast and intricate jig in perfect unison. I watched in pure horror. I could see from the stricture of their trousers that both policemen now revealed an impressive display of balls.

Apologia

These stories raise more issues than can possibly be dealt with in a modest apologia.

For a start there is the claim that the stories revolve around murder. In a majority of the stories, the link with murder is quite tenuous or even non-existent.

I can only focus on the most outstanding issues.

It might be noticed that Bartholomew, in 'The Proof of Miracles', bears a strong resemblance to Stewie Griffin from 'Family Guy.' Both are homicidal, psychopathic toddlers who have designs to murder their mothers. There are at least two differences between Bartholomew and Stewie. One is anatomical and the other is that before 'The Proof of Miracles' begins, Bartholomew has already successfully topped his mother. Lest it be thought that I'd purloined the idea of Bartholomew I should point out that I wrote the story in 1994, several years before 'Family Guy' first aired.

'The Pillar of Sodom' also runs into an age-related issue. The narrator takes revenge on his father by infecting him with HIV and thus puts an end to him. When I wrote the story, HIV was a death sentence but that is no longer the case. Advances in medical science have considerably improved the lot of those with the disease but, at the same time, have undermined the story and rendered it less murdery.

Problems also arise for 'The Nettle Eaters'. At a couple of points in the story the narrative splits into two and provides contradictory accounts of the activities of Mr Peacock, the head of the Independent Police Complaints Commission. I did this to demonstrate how outrageously clever I am. There was no way that anyone else would possibly have thought to do this. Some time after the story was completed I happened to be leafing through 'The Floating Opera' by John Barth and to my horror saw that John Barth had employed the same device of the narrative splitting into two. It wasn't just that it was similar to mine, the structure was exactly the same. John Barth's narratives start with the same sentence, are of equal lengths in two parallel strips down the page and end with the same sentence. I drew consolation from the hope that John Barth had written his version at a later time than I'd written mine. Unfortunately, when I checked up, I found that he'd written his in 1955 whereas I'd written mine in 2004.

There must be a moral in there somewhere.

Printed in Great Britain
by Amazon

16568677R00163